MITZY MCGEE

Mitzy McGee

DIARY
OF A SUPER-GEEK
STUTTERING SONGBIRD

January Joyce

Daddyduckpress

Contents

Additional Works: 1

ACKNOWLEDGMENTS   2

Quote: 3

DEFINITION: 4

Prologue   **5**

SECTION I   **7**

   1 GREMLIN   8

   2 DAMAGED   10

   3 MARNIE   14

   4 SCHOOL   16

   5 RICHARD MCGEE   20

   6 SILVER CREEK   25

   7 THE FIRST BLOWOUT   30

   8 ROCK PUDDING   35

   9 BOOGER EATERS   39

  10 RABID ZOMBIES   42

  11 THE PORCELAIN PONY   45

12 INHERITANCES   49

13 THE TALK   52

SECTION II   **55**

14 BOOK LAND   56

15 PEAS & GRAVY   60

16 SILVER CREEKERS   64

17 THE RED PEN   68

18 BANDANAS   72

19 LIZZY DAULTON   74

20 VANESSA SANTORINI   77

21 LUELLA FARNSWORTH   81

22 THE BEAUFIFUL SARDINE   85

23 ASHLEY AMOS   88

24 CODE III   92

25 FIVE MONTHS LATER   100

SECTION III   **105**

26 CHOCOLATE-PIMPLED RUT   106

27 EXAM ROOM 6   109

28 GALAXY OF GOOFINESS   117

29 THE LIGHT GRAY SEDAN   119

30 ST. THOMAS BAPTIST   124

31 BEAUTY SCHOOL   128

32 SINGING OUTSIDE THE LINES   133

33 PINK-SANDALED GHOUL   136

34 KERN COUNTY FAIR   142

SECTION IV   145

35 TERRANCE DANIEL FORESTER, III   146

36 LEMONS TO CHAMPAGNE   149

37 JUGGLING JIGGLES   153

38 MIRACLE OF THE MACHINE   158

39 SATURDAY NIGHT LIVE   161

40 THE WEREWOLF OF BAKERSFIELD 168

41 MTV VIDEO MUSIC AWARDS   170

42 ELEVENTH GRADE   174

SECTION V   177

43 AFTERMATH OF REGRET   178

44 THREE LITTLE WORDS   181

45 RHINESTONE-STUDDED LIE   183

46 JAILBIRDS   185

47 THE CALL   191

48 COMING CLEAN   200

SECTION VI   207

49 POODLE PUCKER   208

notes   216

Additional Works:

ANATOMY OF A FELON
ANATOMY OF A FELON II -- TAKEOVER
HUNT FOR THE KERN RIVER KILLER
MURDER IN THE 6TH
SHAMEFUL BEINGS
THE 7TH MIRACLE OF OC MERRIWEATHER
I THINK MY CAT IS A TIME-TRAVELING ALIEN

ACKNOWLEDGMENTS

Dedicated to special needs supermom Laura Calvillo and all other caretakers who stand up for and protect those who perceive themselves as being different. And all of the great people at the Stuttering Foundation for all the love you give and the work you do that impacts so many.

Special thanks: Tracy Kelly, Julie Anne Nesselroad Bonderov, Anke Hodenpijl, Ervonne Gorsching, and Cyn Bermudez

Quote:

"Courage doesn't mean you don't get afraid. Courage means you don't let fear stop you."

Bethany Hamilton, American surfer

DEFINITION:

According to the National Stuttering Association at Westutter.org:

- Stuttering is a communication disorder involving disruptions, or "disfluencies," in a person's speech.
- The severity of stuttering varies widely among individuals.
- It's estimated about one percent of the adult population stutters, which equates to almost three million people who stutter in the United States.

Some famous people who stutter: Tiger Woods, Shaquille O'Neil, Adrian Peterson, Mark Anthony, Emily Blunt, Tim Gunn, Steve Harvey, Samuel L. Jackson, Bo Jackson, Earl Jones, Nicole Kidman, Darren Sproles, B. B. King, Marilyn Monroe, Elvis Presley, Charlie Sheen, Ed Sheeran, Carley Simon, Ann McGovern, Jane Seymour, Mell Tillis, Hershel Walker, Winston Churchill, Bruce Willis, and President Joe Biden.

Visit Westutter.com to become enlightened. This book is created to remediate stereotypes and misconceptions and, hopefully, make the world a little better for anyone with a speech disorder or something they perceive themselves as different.

Prologue

February 5, 2011

It's three fifty-two on a crisp, wintery afternoon, and after months of planning, preparation, and practice, I find myself suspended from a thin strand of cable some 170 feet in the air. Looking at the crowd, I estimate Levi's Stadium has around 75,000 anxious spectators. Of course, that's nothing compared to the hundred million viewers watching from the convenience of their couches and barstools worldwide.

Quite frankly, I'm not exactly worried about a strap breaking as I am a wardrobe malfunction or – heaven forbid – one of my backup dancers knocking me off stage (like what happened in 1999 and at the MTV Video Music Awards in 2005). This is one of my biggest moments, and I don't want to be hobbling around, bawling my eyes out when all these people expect a really big show.

So, as I descend to the fifty-yard line – as twenty feet of the most luxurious crêpe de chine billows in the breeze while the underneath harness digs into my thigh fat – I wave to the masses as if I'm floating from a cloud. I disregard the fact the leather bodice feels like it's suffocating me, the urgency that I need to pee (again), and the bug I accidentally swallow as I wave to my fans, supporters, lovers, and haters. I even wave to my mother, wherever Lady Trumpet may be. And I think, *This is it! I made it! This is what we worked our whole lives for!* A melancholy tear slips from my eye as I behold the stadium filled with anxious spectators, giving them my grandest, show-stopping grin.

When my feet hit the ground, a crew of safety technicians un-hitch the rescue hook from my harness before the helicopter lifts and takes flight across the sky. The lights in the stadium go dim, and I'm haloed by a spotlight that accompanies me to the stage. Jimmy Jay's there, as well as my backup dancers and band. Everyone looks anxious and ready.

"You did it, Mitz!" Jimmy Jay calls to me with a gleam in his eye. "Proud of you."

Cupping the microphone in my bedazzled, gloved hand, I'm about to present my first note when I pause to take it all in.

"This is for you, Marnie-mouth," I whisper to the clouds.

Then I blink my lashes into the camera and let them have it as I belt out the opening note of "Millennial Girl," our first chart-topping single that transformed a geeky disregarded reject and set her on the road to becoming a star.

SECTION I

1

GREMLIN

June 1986

O f course, my life didn't start with all that glitz and glamor; I could only wish. No, my journey began in a government housing tract in northeastern Oildale, where the streets had no sidewalks, and the apartment complexes had no playgrounds or yards. Basically, our unit was 610 square feet of muck and yuck. And bugs. I'll never forget the bugs. So, as far back as I can remember, the only glitz and glamor in my life was my mom.

Man, I used to envy her. I mean it. I remember sitting in the passenger seat of her '72 Gremlin, gushing and drooling at her neon blue eyeshadow and how her hair surrounded her face in a whimsical bonnet of curls. Sometimes, she'd catch me staring and admonish me with, "Keep your eyes on the road, baby doll. Ya gotta be on the look-out for the police."

Yeah, those were the days. Mother would be all gussied up in one of her dangerously daring skirts and boots as she headed into town, cupping the steering wheel in one hand and an open beer can or ciggy in the other. She warmed her vocal cords as she drove to one of her favorite tunes from the improvised 8-track in the dash. To me, my mother was the epitome of beauty, talent, and everything good. She was the compilation of a movie star, rock icon, and model rolled into one — no wonder I gushed over her so much.

"Now, you wait here," she'd say when we reached whatever bar, bowling alley, or honkey-tonk hosted karaoke for the night. "Go to sleep. Don't talk to no one and – lord forbid – don't come inside. I catch you getting out of this here car, and I'll tan that hide until the cows jump onto the moon, corral in a bed of cheese, and call it a home. You understand?"

"Yes, Mamma," I responded, knowing better than to ask any questions or register a complaint.

"I'm just gonna go in for a minute. If you gots to pee, there's a cup in the bag (the take-out debris from McDonald's). But you mustn't make a mess, or I'll add scrubbing this here car to your chore list. You got me?"

"Yes, M-m-m-m-mamma."

She applied an additional coat of mascara and then handed me the thick woolly blanket, which kept me warm while protecting me from the scary things that lurked in the night. Then she eased out of the car, locked me inside, and adjusted her skirt so it rode on her thighs at the right length to attract the wrong kind of attention.

She only stumbled once as she headed into the world of men, music, and make-believe. Even though she was slightly inebriated. Even though she was four and a half months pregnant and beginning to show. And even though she left me alone in a dark parking lot with nothing to eat, no toys to play with, and no one to talk to — I watched her walk away from me, exhaling with envy. My mother, Victoria Valentina DeRienzo, was the prettiest woman I had ever seen.

2

DAMAGED

October 1986

T hat's the way it was in those days. Two or three mornings a week (four if she was lucky), my mother got called into work as a housekeeper. I always thought it ironic that she made money cleaning other people's houses when our own place looked like a tornado got a bad case of gas and cut wind all over the place. The cool thing about cleaning other people's houses is all the great stuff she brought home. I can't remember a Christmas or birthday when I didn't receive another kid's cherished sweater, stuffed animal, or already used toy.

Whenever I wasn't in preschool, she brought me with her. I remember walking into these massive structures with double-doored entries, enormous television consoles, elaborate water fountains, and pools in their yards. The best part was that she let me play dress up if nobody was around. I'd venture into the closet of whatever little girl lived there and try on her stuff as if modeling for a fashion show runway. Of course, my mother was too busy to take me to places like Valley Plaza, so playing dress-up with those garments was about as close to a catwalk as I could get. And the shoes! Man-oh-man, I can't tell you how exciting it was to see all the different shoes and imagine what it'd be like to wear them in the real world.

Unfortunately, one day, a family came home and caught me in a full-stage of dress-up. The rich mother was mad. The rich father was mad. The round-faced brother was mad. And the rich little girl was extremely upset when she stormed into the middle of her room with her hands on her hips and her pretty face puckered in a scrunched sneer. That's the day my life changed. That's the day I learned I was different.

"Vicki, what is *she* doing?" The rich mother scolded my mom. "Did you know your thief of a daughter is in here, trying on my precious's things?"

"Nooo," my mother fake gasped as she glared at me. By then, she was eight and a half months pregnant and always in a bad mood. She turned to me (actually, they all turned to me) and snapped, "Mitzy, what are you doing?"

Time muted as they stared at me.

"I-I-I-I-I--"

"Why are you in those clothes? You wanna get me fired?"

"I-I-I am-am-am--"

"Stop that! Give me an answer! What are you doing?"

"I-I-I'm s-s-s--"

"You're what?"

"Sooorry."

"She can't talk!" The rich boy sang. "She can't T, T, T, TALK! She's got a stutter!"

"I-I-I-I'm sorry."

"Say it right," Mother cracked, "or I'll give you a whoopin'!"

"What about punishing her for invading my daughter's room and taking her clothes," the father snapped. "My wife told you, she thought your little heathen's a thief!"

"I don't want her here," the mother cut in. "Just look at her! Her hair's a mess, she reeks as if she hasn't bathed in months, and those teeth have never seen a toothbrush."

"She's. Just. Gross," the daughter added. "I think there's something wrong with her; she's brain-damaged or something."

Mom, please help.

The rich mother sneered at me. "That's what you get for stealing my daughter's things. Sounds like the devil's got ahold of your tongue, little lady!"

Tears welled in my eyes. *Mom!*

"Seriously, I just want a clean house; I don't want my children exposed to all this."

Say something, Mama. Please say something!

"The world's hard enough as it is." The rich mother droned theatrically. "We've worked hard for our status. My husband is a consultant at a very prestigious firm. We moved to this neighborhood to get away from lowlifes and losers. So, if you don't mind, get her out of our house and don't bring her back. That thing," she pointed at me, "isn't welcome here."

"Listen," Mother intervened.

Here it comes! She's gonna yell at them and tell them not to pick on me. She's gonna tell them to "stick it where the sun doesn't shine!"

"Sorry," Mother cooed. "I'm embarrassed. I knew I shouldn't have brought her here. Mitzy started this silly goof-talk a while ago. I tried soap. I tried hot sauce. I even tried slapping some sense into her, but I can't get her to talk right. And with the stealing, I assure you, her discipline will be most severe."

Her fingers dug into my shoulder.

"Ow-o-o-o-www!"

"Shush!" She shook me. "I'm tired of this! You're gonna sit in the car till I'm done!"

She took the rich girl's dress off me in front of the family, then pulled the tee-shirt/underwear-clad me out of the house.

This is one of many instances that happened back then, but don't feel bad for me. You already know I grew up and became a famous rock/pop legend and actress. To date, I have an Emmy nomination, two Oscars, and eight platinum-selling albums, which led to being the halftime entertainer at the Super Bowl. I overcame poverty, abuse, and a lot of bullying to become a   beloved spokesperson and activist. But I didn't do it alone. I had a charismatic force of fury by my side. I had my sister, Marnie.

3

MARNIE

November 1986

Marnie was born on November 22, 1986, and she came out screaming. Actually, she came out screaming, bawling, pooping, and barfing up a lot of goopy foul-smelling stuff. She was a fountain of gross. But in between the barfing, spitting up, farting, and the spigot of boogers that seeped from her nose, she was a cuddly bundle of joy. Actually, she was *my* cuddly bundle of joy because Mother was too busy working out and prepping her nails and hair.

While I rocked Marnie to sleep, Mother did Pilates with a cigarette in her hand. While I changed Marnie's diaper and washed her clothes, Mother whitened her teeth with a newfangled solution from the dollar store. And while I read fairytales to Marnie and rocked her to sleep, Mother set out on the road for a night of barroom adventure.

At first, I resented my mother for abandoning us by leaving us home alone, but I soon felt so enamored with Marnie that those nights and days became treasured folds of my childhood. For the first time in my life, I felt loved.

Marnie didn't care that I talked funny. Marnie wasn't disgusted by my messy hair and tattered clothes. Marnie cherished everything about me. Not only did I feel loved, but for the first time in my life, I experienced a sense of self-worth. So, while Mother gallivanted around town in a never-ending selection of miniskirts and man-hunting wear, I made sure my pudgy, happy terror of a little sister was well taken care of and safe.

4

SCHOOL

October 1988

Marnie was cute and cuddly but also a big fat pain in the you-know-what — let me tell you. She did things that drove me crazy. If I donned my thrift store birthday gloves, she wanted to wear them. She'd scamper across the room, screaming and squealing until I gave them to her. Then she'd try them on, realize they didn't fit, and discard them on the floor. If I bathed, she'd crawl inside with me and accidentally pee (or poop) in the water. I don't know if the warm water relaxed her or what, but once her beefy little behind settled into the tub, she turned into a fart-bursting bubble machine. And it didn't matter if I was eating a frozen pancake, bag of chips, bologna sandwich, or an old stale French fry that I found on the couch; Marnie squawked and wanted dibs. So, I cleaned the bathwater and bathed her, handed her my gloves, and gave her the first bite of whatever I ate because Marnie and me *was* sisters, and that's what sisters do.

By the time Marnie turned two, I'd missed so much school the authorities threatened to report Mother to child protective services. I wouldn't have minded a foster parent who actually did some of the chores, but the concept of Marnie and I being separated had me more than a little on edge. That's when Mrs. Dunlop (the grandmotherly type from the apartment next door) began looking after Marnie when Mother and I were busy. Fortunately for Marnie and me, that was nearly every school day. For the first time in my life, I regularly attended class.

First grade was a big whopping change in my life. I knew my letters, numbers, and easy math (such as single-digit addition and subtraction), but I sucked at pretty much everything else. Besides that, I'd been called too many names, spat on, ridiculed, yelled at, and forced to eat hot sauce on so many occasions that I no longer wanted the abuse. I went to class but just sat at my desk and remained numb.

Most kids thought I was shy. Some thought I was stuck up or full of myself. One kid said something was wrong with me, and then a rumor went around that I was born with a teeny tongue and a mutilated voice box. I had to be there, so – quite frankly – I was fine and dandy with that. I was fine and dandy for being an outcast over an embarrassing oral mutation as long as they left me alone. Unfortunately, school personnel saw through my charade.

"Does anyone know the answer?" Mrs. Taylor queried as she scribbled an equation on the chalkboard. She turned to face us, and a half dozen hands shot in the air.

"Mitzy, would you like to give it a try?"

I shook my head and said nothing.

"Come on; I'm sure you'll do well."

I shook my head again.

"There's no such thing as a wrong answer in my class. Effort is the..."

Stop! Would you stop? Ask someone else. I'm a cyborg from another planet. I'm a freak. I'm a stupid freak who can't talk right.

"Please try."

My classmates murmured.

"Instead of saying the answer, you come up here and jot it on the board?"

My shoes solemnly slid across the linoleum as I lumbered to the chalkboard and scribbled 7 in the answer column.

"Nice," Mrs. Taylor decreed, "I'm impressed."

When I returned to my seat, my heart felt something unusual and strange. For the first time since I started school, I had a small, tiny inkling of feeling not so troll-like.

Three days later, Mrs. Taylor stopped me as I approached my seat. "Mitzy, put your things away. You need to report to the principal's office."

I had no clue why I'd been summoned like that. My stomach ate my brain while my heart fell to the floor in a gelatinous heap. I felt terrified as I dragged my feet to the scary, forbidden place at the front of the school.

"Miss DeRienzo," Principal Trowers greeted, "come in. Make yourself comfortable. I'd like you to meet a few of my associates."

Four primly dressed grownups sat in the room.

"Your mother indicated she couldn't attend this conference, so we'll introduce ourselves and draw up a plan to see how we can help."

I sat in silence as they went around and introduced themselves. When Miss Ocampo (a young, attractive Filipino-American lady) introduced herself, she indicated was my new speech therapist. I didn't know what a speech therapist was, so my face scrunched.

"That means," she smiled, "instead of going to class, you'll come to my office a couple of mornings a week and practice sound patterns."

Don't say anything. No one can help. I'm deformed. I'm damaged. I'm different. I'm dumb. I'm ugly and smelly and dirty and dumb.

My fingers cemented. My throat barricaded a storm of anguish. As I fought an eruption of ache, the grownups appeared wounded. I tried my best to hold it in, but I mistakenly released an obnoxious walrus yelp.

Miss Ocampo's eyes draped with concern. "What's going on?"

Don't say anything!

"Please tell me why you're upset."

I looked down.

"Mitzy, we've been in contact with your mother. We know you can talk. We're just not sure why you choose to remain silent."

"I'm d-d-d-damaged."

"Who told you something so terrible? That's untrue." Miss Ocampo reached over and cradled my hand. "Just like everyone has different hair textures, we all have different textures and patterns of speech."

It was the first time someone mentioned my stutter with compassion. Tears escaped me.

"Ah, come here." She knelt in front of me with open arms.

I hugged her. I actually hugged her. I hugged this strange, beautiful woman in front of everyone.

"I'll make it fun; I promise," she assured. "You're not in this alone."

5

RICHARD MCGEE

September 1991

Two weeks into the fourth grade, I returned from school and walked into turmoil. The apartment had been partially cleaned while Mother bustled about in a frenzy.

"Mitzy, get in here. Hurry, put your things away, and get in here. Start drying dishes and stacking them on the shelves."

I barely took two steps when she snapped, "In your room! Your things go in your room!"

She dashed out of the kitchen, through the small living area, and out the front door, toting two trash bags and an armful of pizza boxes. A minute and forty seconds later, she scoured the remaining pots and pans, wiped down the cabinet doors, and scrubbed the floor on her hands and knees.

"Is the a-a-apartment manager coming for another i-i-inspection?"

"No, listen..." Her eyes lit with crazed calamity, and a part of me wondered if she was on drugs. "I met someone. A man friend. He's very nice, and I've invited him here for dinner tomorrow night. I want the place spic and span and the both of you on your best behavior."

Although Mother drank, smoked, cussed, and ate a lot of junk food, she spent most of her time prepping and preparing to land "a good one." Part of me wondered if this guy would be like the long list of losers who ended up hitting her, spent all day snoring on the couch, or left in handcuffs when the police came.

As Mother rehung the blinds, fluffed the couch cushions, and vacuumed the upholstery, I picked up Marnie from Mrs. Dunlop's. After we collected the discarded cigarette butts and stray candy wrappers from behind the couch, we ventured to our room to tidy our things. An hour or so later, Marnie and I took a bath wherein I shampooed and conditioned her hair, removing all the cobwebs and dried food clumps. And then we brushed our teeth with brand-new toothbrushes before going to sleep.

A couple of hours later (sometime in the middle of the night), I awoke to a rustle of swooshes and clicks.

"You didn't cut her nails!" Mother spat as she hovered over Marnie, clasping nail clippers. "They're filthy and long. They look like bat claws."

I pretended to sleep.

"Mitzy, I'm serious. You should have got this done."

I remained still.

"My friend's gonna show up around four. You and your sister need to be on your best behavior. This is important. This guy has no criminal record and a good-paying job. Plus, he's handsome. He's everything I've hoped for, and you girls better not mess it up."

I couldn't sleep that night, thinking about the long list of losers she'd brought into our lives. *I hope he won't yell at me; I hate it when they yell at me. I hope he doesn't call me names and pick on me like the others. Please, God, please. Make him not come. Let him get arrested for driving drunk or stealing. Let him race his car and crash into a cow field. Maybe he can do the wrong drugs and fall asleep in a dirty bathroom stall. Have him go to his other girlfriend's house.*

* * *

The next day in class, my stomach churned and chewed with worry. I couldn't get it out of my head. Mother had never been so frantic about having the apartment clean. More than anything, I dreaded going home and hearing the infamous knock on the door. More than anything, I didn't want to meet this strange, scary monster.

When that knock happened at 4:06 p.m., Mother looked and acted like an entirely different person. Whatever drug she was on, I liked it. Her makeup was light. Her outfit: modest. Her attitude: wholesome. Her manner: nice. As Marnie and I sat on the couch in our brand-new dresses (with the tags tucked in so they could be returned), Mother sprang from the couch and inhaled deeply before she swung the door open.

The man on the walkway out front looked nothing like the others she scrounged up and brought home. That man was Richard McGee.

*   *   *

Richard McGee stood 6'2, lean, and wore a button-down shirt and pressed jeans. Before he walked in, he handed Mother a flower bouquet wrapped in green cellophane.

"Oh, thank you," Mother gushed in her sweetest sugar voice. "Come in, come in; I'd like you to meet my little angels."

It was the first time I heard my mother call us "angels," look at us that way, or talk about me as if I were appreciated. I sat astonished.

Richard entered the room carrying gift bags. Instead of kicking us girls off the couch so that he had a comfortable place to sit. Instead of looking for a nasty place to spit his chew. Instead of burping and walking to the refrigerator to help himself to another beer. And instead of barking, "Kids need to be outside," Richard handed one gift bag to Marnie and the other to me.

Marnie accepted the brightly decorated tote, opened it, and immediately squealed. Inside, she found a brand-new baby doll that wet its diaper. From that moment on, she's been smitten. I, on the other hand, appreciated that he brought me a miniature doctor's stethoscope; nevertheless, it took me a little time to warm up to this strange Richard person.

While Marnie gushed and drooled over Richard during an actual home-cooked meal of spaghetti, I seethed in my seat. I gave him dirty looks and kicked his leg. I even spilled soda on his jeans.

"Mitzy," Mother scolded in an embellished tone, "please be careful. Respect our guest."

"I'm so sorry, Richard. She's... She's... She's a difficult child. She's different, as you can see. And she's—"

"Shy and protective of her sister," Richard intervened. "I can appreciate that. I'm a stranger in her home. It may take time for her to warm up. Give her a chance; I'm not going anywhere."

Marnie hopped on his lap and inspected the inside of his ears. Richard chuckled in response. And then Marnie stood on his legs to check the top of his head to see if he had lice or a dandruff problem.

"Get down!" Mother scolded. "That's—"

"Normal childhood curiosity for a kid her age. Let it go."

Mother silenced. She actually shut her mouth and listened. That's when I decided I hated this guy. He was too nice, and I knew it would only lead to disaster. I'd already been through Mother's procession of lowlifes and losers, who pretended to be supportive at first, then turned into yelling machines, complaining machines, and other sorts of fakery who had no interest in being around kids. Therefore, I decided to do something shocking and repulsive, something that would scare away the most ardent suitor. I did the one thing that would cast him out of my life. I spoke.

"R-R-R-Richard," I began.

It immediately got their attention.

My mother's jaw dropped as her eyeballs shriveled into the backs of their sockets. It was the first time she witnessed me speak in front of others in a little over eighteen months.

"I-I-I-I don't want you here."

"Mitzy!" Her fist slammed the tabletop. "How dare you insult our guest! What'd I say about talking? If you can't talk right, don't—"

"Excuse me," Richard interrupted. "In my house, we don't raise our voices at the table. She should be allowed to express what she feels. And, most importantly, I hope you weren't going to say anything derogatory about her speech. That could be damaging and make it worse."

And then this Richard stranger directed his attention to me. "At the end of the night, if you don't want me to return here, I won't. I'll respect your opinion. But I want you to understand your mother and I have taken a liking to each other. I'm a widower. My wife was hit by a drunk driver, leaving my children and me feeling rather alone. If this works out with your mother and me, I'd like to make you and your sister a part of our family. One thing you, your sister here, and your mother should know: in my world, in my home, in my life, children *always* come first."

Marnie hugged Richard with so much enthusiasm she ripped out a machine-gun-rattle fart. Mother produced a weary grin as an invisible cloud of stink infiltrated the room. While I sat there and made the monumental decision – probably the biggest decision I made in my life – to give this Richard person a chance. Little did I know:

1. Within three days, Marnie would start calling him "Daddy."
2. Two weeks later, they wed in Las Vegas, bringing all us kids with them.
3. Richard's kids (Jimmy Jay and Leiann) became lifelong friends and the true definition of siblings.
4. After the wedding, we moved into Richard's four-bedroom house in Silver Creek.
5. Mom suddenly turned into a mother (well, sort of).
6. And that Richard would eventually adopt Marnie and me and become the world's greatest Dad.

6

SILVER CREEK

October, 1991

S ilver Creek Estates is a neighborhood smack dab in the middle of southwest Bakersfield. Encompassing parks, community pools, and a reputable school, Silver Creek hosts an assortment of family activities.

The third time I journeyed there, all my belongings were packed in a cardboard box in the cargo bed of Richard's truck while Marnie and I sat inside the soft, comfy interior. As I gazed out the window, I saw kids riding bicycles, scooters, and skates. Some played hopscotch. Some sank rims in basketball hoops while others milled around lawns, leisurely having a good time. Compared to our apartment in Oildale, it looked like a make-believe land from television. It looked fun.

In Oildale, I never felt like a part of the community. I'd always been the odd smelly imp everyone cast aside. My stutter made me an outcast because I'd been conditioned to keep quiet. I didn't speak, so I didn't socialize. Therefore, I didn't spend my weekends digging in trenches or chucking rocks against the old metal dumpster in the parking lot. Instead, I remained banished to my room, where I had no one besides my sister. Moving to Silver Creek changed everything.

I get to live here! I marveled as Richard pulled into the drive-way. *No more cockroaches scampering across the floor. No more apartment managers pounding on the door. No neighbors accusing Mother of stealing. No waking to the sound of gunshots. No stepping over needles in the parking lot. No more being the lowlifes of the block.*

Naturally, I'd been to Richard's house. Marnie and I had visited twice to get acquainted with our new living arrangements. During those times, I remember my complete shock when I saw the shiny appliances that encompassed the kitchen. I remember sitting on the stain-free couch with no springs poking my thighs. But most of all, I remember his restrooms.

The bathrooms in that house were luxurious and clean; they didn't reek like urine, and the shower wasn't coated in unidentifiable space-like substances. I know it sounds silly, but I clearly remember sitting on the toilet seat, feeling privileged. *I get to pee here! I get to pee in Richard's bathroom! I'm peeing in this super-fancy, beautiful place!*

Of course, I now know that house was just a modest middle-income residence in an affordable neighborhood. Richard McGee wasn't a filthy-rich tycoon with the money and means to buy every-thing he wanted, but a down-to-earth regular schmo who broke his back to support his family and the woman he loved. But that first day, walking into the house and putting our things in the new room, I felt like we won the lottery.

*   *   *

I don't remember seeing much of Jimmy Jay when we moved in. He probably went to a friend's house or stayed out of the shuffle by hibernating in his room. Maybe he had a problem with his dad marry-ing our mom. Maybe he didn't want us there. I don't know. All I knew was that Jimmy Jay was a new breed of different, even back then.

While most of the boys around town had shaved heads and combed-over bangs, Jimmy Jay sported a mullet — an actual mullet. I'd never seen anyone with a mullet. Back then, I didn't even know they existed. But there he was, walking, talking, and becoming my brother with a long gleaming mane that streamed down his back while the hair on the sides of his head appeared to have been hacked short by a lawn-mower. It looked like whoever cut his hair got frustrated and quit.

To this day, I chuckle at the recollection. But, hey, who am I to talk about another person's hairstyle when my own strands were a greasy, dandruff-filled cluster of clumps. Okay, yeah, I know I was a freak. I was the freak everyone made fun of. I was the freak who invaded *his* home. But, still, I couldn't get over the fact there was something unusual about my new so-called "brother."

Leiann, on the other hand, was an entirely different story. "I hope you like it," she gushed as she opened the door to our room, which used to be hers before she relocated to the study.

Inside, I saw a window overlooking a frolicking Cypress covered in blooms, an adult-sized rocking chair, and a wooden bunk bed. The thing that stole my breath, however, was the mural. All four walls were covered in a mosaic of magic and make-believe. It was breathtaking; it could have graced an amusement park ride or been displayed at a museum. My heart melted. Mere words couldn't define its beauty.

Leiann must have known what I was thinking. "My mother painted it when I was around your age. I had a thing for fairies and forests back then. Took her weeks to complete. I hope it gives you the same happiness it gave me."

I'd never seen a painting like that. I never knew art could emote such a feeling. The fairies, trees, flowers, and bees relayed messages of faith, tolerance, courage, and love. Marnie clasped her hands against her chest with her breath stuck.

"Oh, I got sheets for your beds with nighties and matching slip-pers. I couldn't resist; I hope I got the right sizes."

Marnie couldn't take it any longer. She dashed over and wrapped her fat, chunky arms around Leiann's leg.

"Aww, you're so adorable."

Marnie nodded in agreement.

"Now, let me show you how to work the blinds. Oh, and I got a hold of a nightlight shaped like a butterfly. I thought you'd want a nightlight, being new to the place and all."

Marnie didn't respond. It appeared as though she wanted another compliment.

"Don't worry, sweetie. It will feel like home in no time. There's some of my toys in the toy chest." She chuckled. "I outgrew them years ago, so you can keep whatever you like."

Marnie danced on her toes; she liked the concept of toys.

"Oh, you're so sweet. I can't get over how precious you are."

Leiann started to walk out but stopped, turned, and gazed into Marnie's big, beautiful brown eyes.

"If you get scared, I'll leave my door open so you can come an' bunk with me. I don't know if you want that. Maybe I should ask your mom."

"No," Marnie grunted in a death growl.

All this time, I thought Leiann would resent us for moving in. I thought she'd mock me for being a stupid, ugly freak. *It's coming,* I kept thinking. *She likes Marnie but is only kind to me because she hasn't heard my stutter. Once she hears how I talk, she will forget about being my sister.*

Without even thinking about it, I spontaneously blurted, "I-I-I-I hate the-the-the mural. It's d-d-d-d-dumb!" *Why'd I do that? Why'd I say something so horrible?*

"Listen, you two." Leiann reeled us into her soft, cocoa butter-scented embrace. "I've wanted a little sister my entire life. I know you come with unique personalities and experiences; that's okay. That's what makes you — you. When it comes to art or pajamas or how comfortable we are talking in front of others, we all have our ways. We're different."

She reached over to cup my chin in her hand, but I jumped back. *She's gonna slap me!*

Leiann stopped short when she saw me duck as if to avoid an assault. She stood open-mouthed for a second or two before she continued, "As I said, I always wanted a little sister. Now my dad gets married, and I have two."

She wrapped us in a three-way hug.

"Me, me, me," Marnie chimed, trying to hog the attention.

"This is gonna be a good thing," Leiann declared with a scrunched nose. "We'll be sisters for the rest of our lives."

I felt so relieved she didn't hit me and guilty because I lied about the mural that I didn't notice the something-stinks expression on Leiann's face.

"But for now," she stated squeamishly, "I'd like to know when's the last time either of you smelly bellies had a bath?"

7

THE FIRST BLOWOUT

The evening of October 4, 1991

The next hour or so went off without drama. After Marnie and I
bathed, we played in our room until Richard came and tucked us
into bed. Tucking us into bed consisted of sitting in the antique
rocking chair and reading a story. It was the first time Marnie and
I experienced anything like that. Richard narrated the characters in a
way that made the tale magical. Once Richard turned the last page, he
pulled our covers to our chins before planting peck kisses on each of
our foreheads.

"Good night, princess," he said as he leaned over me, donning
his correctional officer's uniform. "I hope you enjoyed your first day
in your new digs. Maybe tomorrow, you can try talking a bit — if
you're comfortable. I promise I won't say anything about your stutter.
Believe it or not, I had a stutter when I was your age. It's nothing to be
ashamed of."

He paused to wait for my response, but I said nothing.

"I'll be 10-9 while I work the night shift, but I'll 10-19 home
bright and early in the morning so your mother and I can take you to
school. Sleep well."

I didn't say anything in response. I wasn't sure if I liked Richard and his quirky correctional officer jargon. I especially didn't like the concept of going to a new school.

"Good night, princess," he said to Marnie.

"Good night, Daddy," she replied, all cherub-like and sincere.

And then she said something that astounded me and had my mind reeling. "I love you."

Richard turned off the light, leaving Marnie and me basking in the illuminated enchantment of our new lives.

"Mitzy," Marnie whispered a few seconds later, "I like it here."

"I like it here, t-t-t-t-too, M-Marnie," I replied. "G-g-g-g-g-good night."

The sound of rustling covers diminished as Marnie floated into the land little girls go when they rested contentedly. Then, just like always, I heard the ghoulish wheezes and snorts of her breathing.

I tried to sleep, but the quieter it got, the louder my thoughts spun. *I have to go to a new school. I don't like school; I especially don't like going to a new school. They'll make fun of me, and I'll never have friends.* But under the layers of worry and shame, my conscience tried to re-press something heavier. *Why did you treat Leiann like that? It's mean and untrue.*

After a while, I couldn't take it anymore. Quietly and remorse-fully, I climbed from the top bunk, tiptoed across the room, and snuck out the door. I needed to find Leiann and tell her I adored the mural and appreciated everything she had done. But as I padded across the upper landing, I overheard a commotion from downstairs.

"The heck, you're not!" Leiann snapped.

"Watch your mouth," Mother snapped back. "Don't you dare speak to me that way! I (something indiscernible)."

"I'll speak to you whatever way I want. Who do you think you are? You're not *my* mother; *my* mother would never dress like that or (something else indiscernible). You're not going to come in here, invade my life, and tell me what to do."

Step by step, I crept down the staircase to eavesdrop without being heard.

"And if you think you're gonna go out and abandon your kids like that, you're sadly mistaken."

"I'm not abandoning anyone," Mother lashed back. "Don't be ridiculous! I'm just going out for a bit."

"No, you're not. You leave, and I'll tell my dad. I'll tell him how you called around and couldn't wait to get out the door."

"There's nothing wrong with karaoke. Stop making a fuss. You make me sound like a criminal or something. I'm just stepping out for a minute. Richard knows I go to karaoke; he loves my voice."

"You're a terrible mother."

"How *dare* you speak to me that way!"

"Just sayin' what I see. You've been here, what, one whole day, and I haven't seen you do squat for them."

"I cooked dinner. I made sure they were fed and—"

"You slapped together turkey sandwiches. Yeah, I'll give you credit for that. But you didn't help them unpack or give them two seconds of your time. No, you were too busy fussing with your things and fixing your nails. You had all the time in the world to put your clothes away and claim the downstairs restroom as your own. You made sure your fragrances lined the countertop. You even chatted with your friends, but what about your kids?"

"Check that attitude; you won't tell me what to do. Just because you're fifteen doesn't mean you can be rude."

"So, I'm fifteen. What's your excuse?"

"WHAT?"

"I speak my mind 'cause that's what kids my age do. What's your—"

"Get out of my way. I'm going out, and you're not going to stop me."

"You step one foot out that door, and I'll tell my father you hit them."

"WHAT are you talking about?"

"I think you hit them. I think you slap their faces and can only imagine what else you do. Man, if my father found out, it'd put an end to your relationship."

End the relationship? I fretted. *No!!! I don't want that!*

"He's a correctional officer, and correctional officers have no sympathy for child abusers, most especially my dad."

Marnie's happy here. I'm happy here. I like Richard and Leiann and this house. I even like Jimmy Jay.

"He'll kick you out and get a divorce."

No, please! Not a divorce!

"I can punish them how I—"

"That little girl's just nine. What kind of savage slaps her own—"

"What'd you call me?"

"A savage, savage."

"Well," Mother interrupted, "I think you're the—"

"S-S-S-Stop!" I bellowed as I descended the remaining steps. "Please do not fight. I d-d-d-don't want to fight. I-I-I—"

The sound of a car honking emanated from the driveway out front.

Leiann and Mother looked at each other for a moment of uncertainty.

"Just go," Leiann spat.

"Get back to bed," Mother chimed as she gave me an overly enthusiastic, exaggerated hug. Then, she turned and darted out the doorway, wearing her beloved animal-print cowboy pants, a sequined shirt, and red velvet boots.

Leiann stood stunned as she gazed down at me.

"I-I-I-I-I-I w-w-w-wanted to tell you that I'm sorry," I gushed as I crumpled into her arms.

"You don't need to apologize; that didn't involve you."

"About the m-m-mural." *There, it felt good to get it off my chest.* "I lied. I l-l-love it."

"Oh, Mitzy!"

Leiann took a deep breath and led me to the ottoman, where we sank into the plush, cushiony island in the middle of the room. A room that was meticulously decorated. A room adorned with family pictures and wall plaques. A haven that felt peaceful and serene, where the walls whispered tales of another woman's affection for her family. A vault of happy memories.

"Moving can be cruddy. I know it's hard to lose your friends and uproot your life. You've been through so much. But the most important thing right now is that you're comfortable talking with me."

She lifted my chin and peered into my eyes.

"Proud of you, Mitz."

Then she hugged me. She hugged me in a way that felt safe and accepted. She hugged me in a way I'd ached for my entire life. She hugged me like I'd seen in movies, the way other mothers hug their little girls. Her embrace felt as though a ladle of hope poured into my chest, filling my heart with assurance.

It was a crazy ending to a bizarre day. Leiann will always be my greatest role model and source of support. As I nestled back into bed – as I pulled up the sleek, satin-lined bedcover and basked in the effervescence of the room – little did I know:

1. The battle for house matriarch would be a brutal one.
2. Their fighting continued for the next three years.
3. Mother tormented Leiann with a never-ending barrage of criticisms, complaints, and ceaseless demands.
4. Richard (mesmerized by Mother's good looks and whatever else he saw in her) grew weary of his position as mediator.
5. Two days after she graduated from high school, Leiann enlisted in the Marines, leaving me heartbroken and abandoned.
6. My second chart-topping single, *Heroes Like Leiann*, not only stayed on the Top 10 list for weeks; it made "Leiann" a household word.

8

ROCK PUDDING

October 7, 1991

Monday morning, Marnie and I slid into the backseat of Richard's truck, feeling shaky. Actually, I was scared out of my wits. While we passed rows of perfectly manicured lawns along the drive to our new school, Richard gave us a correctional officer's form of pep talk.

"Okay, kiddos, the first day of school. Ya gotta try and show no fear. In prison, we always get first-timers who are afraid, and it shows. When the pack sees fear, they go for blood. So, you gotta play it off. Play it cool. Pretend you belong there. Pretend like you own the place. Act like you're top dog and aren't afraid to call the shots."

"Okay," I muttered.

"Sure, Daddy," Marnie dittoed.

"Better not get any phone calls you start any trouble," Mother intervened. "I planned a busy day and don't want to get called to the office."

"O-o-o-okay."

"Na," Richard interjected, "I'd rather you take care of business on your first day than let a bully or spoiled badger get away with anything."

"You bet!" Marnie chirped.

"Put them in check. Show 'em kids whose boss, but I want you to make friends. Most importantly," he turned in his seat to face me, "no standing down on talking. Talk, and if they say anything about your stutter, give 'em a cold squint of stink eye."

"O-okay."

Even though Richard's pep talk leaned a little on the side of an old-time guard's mentality, it was a thousand times better than Mother's *Don't Get in Trouble* lecture.

Richard found an available space in visitor's parking. Once he parked, Richard (in his correctional officer's uniform with a cover-shirt on top) and Mother (in a tank top and skintight jeans) escorted Marnie and me to the office.

Marnie's paperwork had already been completed. My little sister had officially enrolled in kindergarten. We stood at the gate and took pictures. We moved to the door of her classroom and took pictures. And we walked inside Marnie's classroom, where Marnie posed, displaying her brand-new backpack and tote.

When we returned to the office, it took a while for the secretary to process my papers. The entire time we waited, Richard held Mother's hand as if he didn't have any place better to be.

* * *

"Look," a girl in a cute sweater announced when I entered my classroom, "a new person!"

All the kids simultaneously turned in their seats and expectantly paused. But I didn't talk even though I promised Leiann and Richard I would. As usual, I remained silent.

"Here," a brown-haired boy called from the third row, "you can sit next to me." He smiled widely, and I wondered if it was a setup or a ploy.

"Hi," a pony-tail-haired girl greeted me as I passed her desk.

I remained silent as I weaved between landmines of desks.

"Hold it," Miss Dorsey called to me. "You're assigned right there in that available seat."

Appraising the situation, I surmised the fourth-row desk was smack dab in the center of the classroom. Smack dab center wasn't my thing; I'm more of a back corner, by the reading shelves kind of gal. I ignored her as I proceeded to the back of the room.

"Stop,'" Miss Dorsey snapped, "can you hear me?"

Remaining stubborn, I slid into the seat.

"Can. You. Hear. Me?" she snapped louder.

I said nothing.

"Mitzy," she double-checked my name on the admittance paper-work, "DeRienzo. Last chance. Answer the question!"

"I-I-I-I-I did h-h-h-hear you-you," I retorted. "I-I-I-I just don't like being in the middle of the r-r-r-room."

"Okay," she relayed, visibly taken aback. "Put your things away, and we'll continue our lesson."

Why'd I talk? Now they know. Now they know about my stutter.

I wish I could go back to nine-year-old me and tell myself that if I spoke to my classmates, they'd get used to it. Some would empathize with my situation, and I'd make friends. I wish I could tell myself that every person there had their own insecurities. Each person struggled with issues that made them feel different. I'd tell myself that giving them a chance would be giving myself a chance as well.

As Miss Dorsey scribbled sentences on the chalkboard, all twenty-seven classmates swiveled in their seats to get a better look. The way they ogled and stared had me feeling like a zoo attraction. Trying my best to ignore them, I focused on a graffiti message etched into my desktop.

Rock Pudding — what does it mean?

"Did you hear the way she speaks?" Ponytail girl whispered ani-matedly. "She sounds like a broken record."

"She can't talk right," another girl agreed.

There's no such thing as Rock Pudding. This doesn't make sense.

"It's called a 'stutter,'" the boy with the brown hair cut in.

"Sounds like a car-car-cartoon character to me."

"Sounds stupid."

"Yeah, sounds stupid."

Rock Pudding? Maybe it's a new type of snack or candy bar.

"She's probably—"

So that's basically how it went. One minute, I spoke (as I promised Richard and Leiann I would), and for the next four hours and twenty-one minutes, they made fun of me in ways that had nothing to do with my speech disorder. All I did was sit and stare at those two words for hours.

I just wanted to fit in. I wanted to make friends. I wanted to be normal. But the way they ridiculed me and talked about me made me feel like an outcast. Even the girl with the crud-caked teeth and orangey-red face plastered in sores got in on the whispers.

I can't leave. I can't jump up and run out of the classroom. If I go to the office, Mother will be furious. I wish it would go away. I wish I were invisible.

Hour by hour, lesson by lesson, I tried to ignore my surroundings as my thoughts spun. *I can hear what they're thinking. Even when they don't say it out loud, I know they won't give me a chance. All they see are my flaws.*

After lunch, I reseated myself and returned to stewing. *I'll never have friends. Mother has friends. Lots of friends. So many friends. They call all the time. Sometimes, they visit and lend money. She has people who appreciate everything she does. Why can't I be like her? Why did God make me a person nobody loves? Why would somebody write this? Why did somebody carve Rock Pudding into this desk? What does it mean?*

9

BOOGER EATERS

Mid-October 1991

As usual, Mother was late picking me up. Marnie got out of class two hours before me, and Mother quickly grew weary of making repetitive trips. I thought about trekking along the sidewalk and trying to locate the house on my own, but with my terrible sense of direction and the strange people around the office, I decided to find a quiet hiding place where I could wait. When you have a parent who's seldom on time, you get pretty good at finding places to hide. Once all the other third and fourth graders got picked up, I turned my attention to a community of ants milling about cracks in the asphalt. I'd given them names and imaginary lives when I heard the rumble of Mother's car pulling into the lot.

"Hurry," she called to me over the loud, lively procession of dance-pop, "I don't have much time."

As soon as I slid into the seat next to Marnie, Mother adjusted the gearshift and sped off.

"Listen," Mother spouted, "I've got places to be and don't want you two getting in the way, so I'm gonna drop you off at the house.

But you gotta be quiet. Richard just got to sleep after working all night and running errands."

As she drove, she intermittently gazed in the rearview mirror to check her appearance.

"So, when I drop you off, go to your room. Stay there until I get home. I should only be gone an hour, maybe two, depending on whether there's tanning beds after yoga. Please don't make a mess; I don't want to clean up your messes all day. And Mitzy—"

Here goes, she's going to ask about my day. She's gonna ask if I like my teacher and if I made any friends.

"Your sister's gotten a nasty little habit of picking her nose." Mother reached for a green-and-white coffee cup and took a long, generous sip from a straw. (My mother used straws so the coffee wouldn't stain her whitened teeth.) "It's sooo gross."

Marnie's eyes flickered with mischief.

"Can you do something about her nose-picking?"

Mother took another sip, adjusted her sunglasses, and replaced the cup in the holder. Of course, she didn't offer to share; Mother wasn't necessarily the sharing type.

"And I swear I saw her eating them. She's eating boogers! It's so gross! She won't stop. I don't know why, but she stopped listening. I think she's doing it to torment me."

Marnie wedged her finger into her left nostril.

"Look! She's doing it again! She's doing it now!" Mother squealed. "Make her stop!"

With her face scrunched in a wily grin, Marnie tilted her head as if it gave her picking finger an advantage.

"Marnie, people can see. Stop that! Mitzy, she won't listen. Make her stop."

The finger in Marnie's nose wiggled with excitement.

"Eeek!" Mother shrieked. "What if someone sees? What if one of my friends sees? This is so embarrassing. And gross. No, vile. That is so *vile.* I swear she must have learned it from Leiann."

"S-S-S-Stop," I whispered because I didn't want Leiann brought into another of Mother's tirades.

As Marnie brought her hand down, her composure morphed to innocence.

"That's a disgusting habit you've picked up, little lady. I think Leiann's a bad influence. You need to stop. If you wanna be beautiful, like me, you gotta…"

As Mother lost track in another tête-à-tête about her favorite subject (herself), Marnie reached between the seats and secretively slid her booger-laden fingertip along Mother's cappuccino straw. It's the first time I witnessed Marnie do something so brazen. I should have scolded her. I should have admonished her. I should have let Mother know what my little sister had done. Instead (and for reasons I couldn't comprehend), I sat back and proceeded to giggle. It just happened. Soon, Marnie joined me, and the two of us became giggle monsters. We laughed at the boogers. We laughed at each other. And we laughed because it had become contagious, and that's what little girls sometimes do.

"Could you quiet down and listen to what I have to say?" Mother reached for her cappuccino and proceeded to drink from the booger straw. "I'm tired of…"

I didn't hear what she said, and I doubt Marnie did either. It had been a stressful twenty-something days of moving, bickering, and trying to find our place in the world. Something about the moment seemed magical. Laughing like that just felt right.

10

RABID ZOMBIES

October 25, 1991

Marnie and I woke every morning and had hot cereal or pancakes before Richard walked or drove us to school. On the days we walked, Marnie preferred to ride atop his shoulders, where she liked to tug on his ears as if he were her Daddy-donkey.

"Today's gonna be the day," Richard would say. "Today's the day they'll see past your stutter and discover what a great person you are. I've got faith. It'll happen soon, princess, and your 10-20 will be A-Okay. It'll happen soon."

"Sure, Richard." In my heart, I knew he wanted me to call him Dad; I just wasn't ready. "I'll t-t-t-try my best," I replied tentatively. After all, Richard had no clue that the other students alienated me and how bad it made me feel.

I had tried, again and again, to get them to like me and was met with cold eyes and complaints. In all actuality, I'd pretty much given up on the idea of making friends, although I wasn't going to tell Richard that. No way. Richard may have been a big bad correctional officer who dealt with some of the most dangerous felons in the state; however, living with him, all I saw was the big-hearted softy. When it came to kids, Richard was all heart. And I, for one, wasn't going to be the one to break it.

"Have a good day, Mitz," Marnie called from the gate. "If anyone gives you a problem, I'll get a jaguar to scratch 'em in the knee."

"That's a 10-22. We're not unleashing jaguars in school. Animal Control would have a field day with that one."

But as Richard jested and Marnie threatened to sic a swarm of rabid zombies on anyone who bothered me, I noticed something off with her skin tone. Maybe she hadn't gotten enough sunlight (I couldn't tell), but she seemed unusually pale.

The bell rang, and I took off towards my classroom. At the desk in the back of the room, my finger traced the same two words as my mind traveled to imaginary places. I daydreamed about a cove in Hawaii, a meadow where I rode magnificent stallions, and a mountain-top perch where I floated amongst clouds.

*   *   *

Sometime around ten, I received a note to report to the office. Part of me wondered if my mother wanted to take me shopping again, where she used me as a decoy while she switched tags. Part of me hoped Leiann dropped off a sack lunch filled with cookies. Never in my imagination did I expect what happened next.

"Miss DeRienzo," Miss Ocampo welcomed me. "How have you been?"

I looked over, and it was her!

"Sorry it took me some time to see you, but it seems we've had a change of plans."

"W-what?"

She ushered me to an office with a desk topped with boxes.

"I received a promotion of sorts. Instead of working part-time and helping a few schools, I've accepted a full-time placement with the district."

"W-w-w-what?"

"I'm back to being your speech therapist."

I lunged across the boxes and hugged her.

"You'll report to my office three or four days a week."

I'd never heard a more beautiful sound.

"If you don't mind, that is." She smiled in her beautiful way. "I promise I'll make it fun."

11

THE PORCELAIN PONY

October 31, 1991

Marnie and I settled into our new routine, which seemed to improve by the day. Mom was mom: she drank in excess, smoked in excess, and conspired to keep her intricate web of secrets away from Richard. As soon as Richard backed his truck out of the driveway, Mother returned to her shenanigans. Therefore, all Richard saw was the caretaker who kept the house clean and put dinner on the table. I suppose it's all he needed to be happy.

Leiann and Mom squabbled occasionally, but they did what they could to keep Marnie and me out of the drama. Sometimes, when I lay in bed at night, I recalled their first blowout and how terrified I was of things getting out of hand. More than anything, I wanted Mother and Leiann to get along, Richard to get along, and Jimmy Jay to get along because I really liked my new home. Although I still hadn't made any friends, Silver Creek was a safe place for Marnie and me, and anything safe for my little pork chop had me over the moon.

* * *

That Halloween, we were excited to celebrate our first holiday as a family. It would be our first-time trick or treating where people handed out stuff we wanted to eat. (In our old neighborhood, people passed out the oddest things: baggies of un-popped popcorn, a table-spoon of jellybeans from a dollar store bag, cigarette papers, and even a broken alarm clock.) Halloween was also Jimmy Jay's birthday, so it was destined to be double the fun. The only thing that stood in the way of being great was the fact it involved the strange, peculiar boy who occupied the same house.

What can I say, Jimmy Jay was just weird. I know back then, I was a silent misfit. Therefore, if there's anyone qualified to make that presumption, it was me. I mean, really. We lived in the same house but rarely spoke, even though Jimmy Jay had the next room. He rode his bicycle all day with his friends, then spent the remainder of his time listening to obnoxious, screechy music that made no sense. He wore ruffled shirts and stretchy pants while his mullet grew into a permanent poof. Frankly, he looked like he'd stuck his fingers into an electrical socket and gotten electrified. And he used hair spray. Yeah, back then, Jimmy Jay used *a lot* of hair spray.

Sometimes, I'd catch him listening to the conversation at dinner as he shifted the food around his plate, pretending to be interested. Sometimes, I'd see him sitting on the ottoman in the living room, reading a book, or listening to whatever tape he had in his Walkman. Sometimes, I heard him practicing chords on a worn-down guitar he purchased at a neighborhood garage sale. But most notably, late at night, when everyone slept soundly, I heard soft, subtle weeping from his room.

Every night, he waited. He waited until Richard had gone to work the graveyard shift at the prison. He waited until Mother had gone out or gotten tipsy and crawled into bed in the master bedroom downstairs. He waited until he thought no one heard, and then, quietly and profusely, I heard the torment in his heart. No one told me, but I knew. He wept in heartbreak for the loss of his mom.

She had to be wonderful. Just look at this house. Look at the mural. Look at the way the curtains complement the upholstery. Look at her spice rack, curios, collection of wind chimes, and how everything's arranged with care. She must have been an incredible mother.

In some weird, bizarre, odd sort of way, I realized Sarah McGee, Richard's first wife (the woman whose passion encompassed every painting, picture, piece of furniture, and adornment in that house) had created something so magnificent and serene that she was a better inspiration and mother to me than my own mom.

*   *   *

After pizza, cake, and ice cream – while everyone sat around the patio, waiting for trick or treating to begin – I noticed Jimmy Jay had done another of his disappearing acts. He skipped out again. No one seemed to notice (because that's what he always did) but me. Marnie fluttered along the grass, entertaining Richard and Mother in her fairy princess costume. Leiann sewed last-minute sequins on Marnie's wings while I sat on a bench in my Smurf garb. That's when I saw Jimmy Jay's hair poof through the window in the kitchen. Don't know why, but I got up and investigated.

The muffled stream of sniffles led the way. Jimmy Jay sat on the living room ottoman, cradling a porcelain pony. Without asking permission, I sat next to him.

"D-d-d-don't worry," I ventured, "no one knows you're h-h-here."

Jimmy Jay turned away and didn't respond.

"I know you miss her."

He shook his head.

"She m-m-must have been awesome."

He shook his head again.

"Is that hers?"

"She liked it a lot," he sighed.

"This might be hard for you to b-b-believe..."

He looked at me inquisitively.

"... but my mother s-sucks."

"No, kidding!"

He chuckled, and I chuckled with him.

"I'm serious. My M-m-m-mom uses deodorant in-between her-her-her boobs, so her cleavage d-d-d-d-doesn't stink like old cheese."

Jimmy Jay wiped his eye with the back of his hand, then he turned towards me with eyes lit in astonishment.

"Yeah, and I once saw her steal from a hospital donation bucket. In fact, when she goes to friend's h-h-h-h-houses, she takes the change she finds in their-their c-c-c-couch cushions."

Jimmy Jay couldn't help it; his face beamed as he snickered.

"A-and don't tell anyone I t-t-t-told you, but one time I actually saw her pick up already chewed gum and p-p-put it into her mouth."

"Was it hers?" he gasped.

"Don't know. We were in a restaurant. But I know sh-sh-she's pretty gross. Not like your mom. Y-Y-Y-Your mom must have been-been amazing. I'm sorry she died. I'm sorry a drunk driver wen-went on the road and k-k-k-killed her. It's not fair."

"Yeah," Jimmy Jay looked at me and cracked a compensatory smile, "it's not fair."

We said nothing for a while, which seemed okay. Somehow, the silence wasn't awkward or loud or screaming. I felt comfortable being beside him, and his frilly fluffed hair that sometimes tickled my ears and got tangled in my lashes.

12

INHERITANCES

November 1991

Sometimes, Jimmy Jay's group of friends knocked on the door. Sometimes, they summoned him from the basketball stand by the mailbox. And, sometimes, they remained on their metal steeds and whistled from the street. The Saturday after Halloween was a street-calling kind of occasion.

"Hey, JJ, get your butt out here!"

"Hurry up, McGee, we don't have all day!"

"JJ! JJ!"

This occasion would have been like all the rest. The gangly crew would have ridden to the park or along side streets until they got to the Marketplace, where they milled around, looking for kids to catch up with until they had to leave. It would have been like every other day, except something happened. Something different. Something unusual. Something extraordinarily unusual.

This time, when he heard the call, Jimmy Jay jumped up from the table, where the two of us sat eating pancakes. He grabbed his coat and bolted towards the door when he stopped, turned, and regarded me sitting in my seat. That's when everything changed. That's when

Jimmy Jay spouted the two most momentous words that melded our relationship, forever changing my life.

"Wanna come?"

My heart skidded as the fork fell from my hand. And then, without thinking about it or realizing what the heck I was doing, I replied, "S-sure!"

And the next thing I knew, my feet barreled out the door behind him. I didn't have a bicycle. As a matter of fact, I wasn't sure I knew how to ride a two-wheeler. I didn't know his friends from Adam, yet there I trotted down the pathway as if I didn't have a care in the world — as if I didn't have a stutter.

"Guys, meet my sister," he announced as more of a statement. "Her name's Mitz. She's gonna ride with us. No one's gonna whine. No one's gonna gimme any lip. No one says squat about her."

The three of them looked at me and nodded their heads, each cute in his own way. 2-Tall pursed his lips in a squiggly W. Billy (the one with broken handlebars and a chipped tooth) squinted at me with an accent of swagger. And Chris Lee nodded as he stretched his arm for a fist bump. We waited as Jimmy Jay went to the garage and collected an old bicycle. I didn't know what else to do, so I folded my arms across my chest and tried my best to act cool.

"It's scratched up, and the seat's a little wobbly," Jimmy Jay passed me the handlebars, "but it'll ride."

"O-o-o-okay."

That was it. That's all he said. I stood awkwardly as Jimmy Jay left me with his friends to collect his regular bike. Once my brother closed the garage door, he hopped on the seat, and the next thing I knew, the four of them took off down the street.

So, I did what I ached to do, wanted to do, and needed to do. I hopped up on the seat, put my feet on the pedals, and then face-planted when I tried to make it go. Not a pretty face plant — no, I ended up with dirt, grime, and asphalt crud all over my forehead. I even swallowed a pebble or two. The worst part of it was I couldn't move. I couldn't get out of it. My ankle had jammed behind the pedal, so I was trapped. I lay there with my face eating dirt and my rear end sticking up in the air.

Unfortunately, for Jimmy Jay and the gang, their newest aficionado had never ridden a bike. So, after they swung back and rescued me, they spent the next hour or so acclimating me to the perils of riding a two-wheeler and the even more perilous concept of acceptance.

That's the fantastic way I inherited Jimmy Jay's friends. It's how I joined the crew and became one of the guys.

13

THE TALK

December 1991

Sometime before Christmas, Richard brought Marnie and me out to lunch. Leiann and Jimmy Jay went to an annual church festival with their maternal grandparents (who welcomed us into their family with open arms), while Mother shopped for last-minute gifts, so it was just the three of us in the booth at Black Bear Diner. As we waited for our order to arrive, Marnie used the occasion to play with straws by blowing bubbles in her water.

While we sat there, Richard gave us "the talk."

"What do you two like about living in Silver Creek?" he began.

"The b-b-bathrooms," I blurted without thinking.

"You," Marnie replied flatly, "and finally living with my brother and sister."

It seemed Marnie had forgotten about our existence before moving to Richard's. She never mentioned Mrs. Dunlop, anything about the apartment, or what it was like living amongst species of drug addicts and bugs.

"Well," Richard began.

He reached over and took a sip of water, and I realized his voice edged with anxiety.

No! I fretted. *Don't say you're getting a divorce. Please don't send me back! Please don't send us back! You'll break Marnie's heart. She loves you. In fact, I love you. I never told you that, but I do.*

"This is hard," his voice cracked.

My heart sank.

"I want to use the right words."

"Wha-what, Richard?" I still called him Richard even though I knew he wanted more.

"Well, you two... What I'd like to know is... Can I — I mean, do you want me to... No, look..." He picked up his water glass and took a hearty drink.

Don't say you're getting a divorce. I know my mom and you had that argument. Don't give up on her. She can change. I promise she can change.

He put his glass down and calmly stated, "I'd like to ask your permission to adopt you."

"Y-yes," I blurted. "Yes, of-of-of course."

"What does that mean, Daddy?" Marnie was puzzled.

"It means," he leaned in and gazed into my sister's big, beautiful brown eyes, "that I'd like to be your Daddy permanently."

"You already are my Daddy," she quipped.

"W-W-Why?" I don't know why I asked him that; it didn't make sense. After all, getting a father like Richard was winning the biggest lottery of all time. "Why do you want to be our-our f-f-f-f-father?"

"Because I care about you," Richard responded. "Because I love having a family to come home to after work. Because I work in a place where bad people do so many horrible things, I just want to come home to a nest full of children. Because my first wife died, and I had a big gaping hole in my heart, you've worked wonders in helping me heal. Because I love kids, especially the two of you, and I want to be your father for the rest of our lives."

"Okay, Daddy," Marnie chimed as she wedged the straw inside her nostril.

Looking into Richard's eyes, I realized he meant every single word.

"Okay, Daddy," I said. And then I reached over and hugged this wonderful man as an ocean of happiness welled in his eyes.

SECTION II

AGES TEN TO ELEVEN

14

BOOK LAND

October 1992

E arly in my fifth-grade year, I fell in love with reading. Inside the pages of books, I no longer embodied a scrawny eleven-year-old with crooked teeth, freckles all over the place, and hair that resembled a tumbleweed. In the world between pages, I wasn't shy or intimidated. And I certainly wasn't someone who couldn't speak right. Perhaps that's why I spent so much time in the library.

The library in our school was an oasis from the perils of the playground. The playground was where medieval entrapments tortured innocent children (such as myself) with the dangers of tetherball, dodgeball, and games of ill repute, where large round objects propelled towards my head. The playground was the place where a lot of mistreatment occurred. And the playground was the habitat of the North American gossipmonger. That's why I preferred my comfy spot in the library, next to shelves stacked with great works from great authors. I marveled how writers weaved words that unraveled my brains in spaghetti, turned them to stone, or macraméd them into elaborate ideas.

So, I read stories – a lot of stories – embedding myself in the narrative. I became characters who personified bravery, brawn, adventure, and strife. And I traveled. Man-oh-man, did I travel. I journeyed to places, worlds, and galaxies, where I survived perils and unimaginable feats. That's okay because Book Land kept me safe from the hazards of the real world — the real world, predominately meaning school.

*   *   *

"I don't want *her* in my group," Alyson moaned, wearing her infamous mushed expression.

Alyson Max, the girl in the seat two rows up, objected to Mrs. Napier's grouping for collaborations on marsupials.

"It's not fair. We got stuck with her last time, and she *like* ruined our presentation. She can't speak right, and she's slow. It took her *like* three minutes to say thirty words. It was *like sooo* embarrassing. I still can't--"

"Yeah," Desiree chimed in. Desiree was Alyson's best friend and bully protégée.

"She says *some* words right." Alyson waved her hand. "The way she picks and chooses which words to mess up doesn't make sense. It's weird, as if she's making it up. I think she talks that way to get attention."

"Now you're accusing Miss McGee of fabricating her speech impediment?" Mrs. Napier grumbled. "You two are something else. This project is part of this class. If you can't learn to work together and respect one another, it will reflect in your grade."

"That's, that's…" Desiree scrambled to find the right words.

"Harassment," Alyson vetted, pleased with herself.

"You're right," Mrs. Napier interjected. "That is what you do. For your information, you could learn a thing or two from Mitzy. She's a good student, and she's—"

"What are you talking about?" Alyson snapped. "Mitzy rarely participates in class. I volunteer for *every* answer while she barely contributes a thing. Look at her; she's got the wrong book on her desk. Is that a vampire on the cover?"

The entire class turned my way.

"Why don't you say something about her reading the wrong book?"

Mrs. Napier turned to me with a stern scowl. I closed the cherished classic with an apologetic shrug.

"I don't want to be grouped with her." Alyson's eyes burned into me. "And if you force this, this collaboration, I'm gonna tell my mom."

"Yeah," Desiree triumphed, "her mom's an attorney. She'll call the principal and—"

"Actually," Mrs. Napier cut in, "involving the principal may be a good idea at this point. It's time the—"

"I-I-I-I don't mind doing the work on my-my-my own," I interjected.

Mrs. Napier gazed at me in disbelief.

"Well then, the *three* of you can go to the office and complete your detention together. You'll stay an hour after school each day until the collaboration's complete with the grouping I assigned. And don't worry about contacting your parents; I'll gladly fill them in on your refusal."

The entire class shrank to the size of a dollhouse. The only noise that could be heard was the teacher's low, monotone voice from the next room.

"And if anyone says anything derogatory about Mitzy again, they'll be expelled from class."

Everyone groaned.

Someone lobbed a ball of paper at my head.

"Shall I assign additional reports on bullying?"

"No," Alyson balked.

"Okay, okay," Desiree receded, "we get it."

Desiree defeatedly lowered her head. "I'm, I'm sorry for what I said. Can we just go back to doing a collaboration on Marsupials? I promise I'll get along."

"And you, Miss Max? Are you going to complete the work I assigned?"

I thought Alyson would apologize; it's what any normal, sane person would do. Instead, Alyson marched out of the room with no explanation. All eyes honed on me.

"Oh-oh-oh, I'm going to st-st-stay and do the report. You-you don't have to bother my mom."

For the next hour and thirty minutes, Desiree and I mapped strategies for our presentation. We studied the various classes and species of marsupials, the distinctive characteristics of how they carried their young, and variations in their diet. Neither of us gossiped, boasted, or said anything mean. Neither of us said or did anything that wasn't marsupial-related.

15

PEAS & GRAVY

Mid-November 1992

M arnie stood in the middle of the yard, unpeeling a Band-Aid.
"Don't go in there!" she heeded with a helping of scorching
eyeballs.

"Why?" I gasped. "Did-did-did something happen?"

"Nope." She placed the Band-Aid on her favorite stuffed frog.
"The toilet in Mom's bathroom accidentally overflowed. Stink water
ruined her salts and slippers."

"Ew, gross!"

"Heck yeah! Wasn't my fault; all I did was flush Froggy's poop,
and it got stuck."

"Froggy p-p-p-poops now?"

"Yeah, he got constipated on Mom's tuna casserole, so I gave him
beans to get the poop out."

"How many beans?"

"Three at first, but when I tried to put some back into the bag,
the rest slipped into the toilet bowl."

"Gross, you shouldn't be-be-be playing around toilets."

"I know. Didn't know what to do with the beans and the plastic bag, so I tried to flush 'em before Mom found out."

"Marnie, you can't flush a-a-a plastic bag!"

"Duh, it got stuck."

"Then what happened?"

"I thought about blaming the neighbors. I was gonna say the Andrews (the family she believed took her inflatable ball) flushed a bag of beans, and it came up in Mom's toilet, but I already used that excuse when I flushed a chicken pot pie last week. So, I covered it with a heap of toilet paper so she wouldn't find out. The toilet paper got soggy, so I tried flushing again, and water flowed all over the place."

"Maybe you shouldn't have f-f-f-f-flushed so many times."

"I may have got carried away."

Marnie grimaced, and I noticed she looked pale again.

"So, w-what happened to Froggy?"

"Mom got mad and knocked him out of my hand. I think she wanted to hurt me too, but... You know."

"Yeah, I know."

Several weeks before, our parents separated for a few nights after a major blowout. Mother lost her temper and slapped me for inadvertently locking her bedroom door. She flipped out because she couldn't access her purse for karaoke night. Richard was fine with karaoke, but he had a definite problem with striking a child. They got into a fight — A Big One. Mother said stuff about taking us to a hotel and suing Richard for child support, indicating she'd get half his paycheck. Richard told her she was free to leave and support herself, but *his* daughters weren't going anywhere that wasn't safe. That's when Richard did something amazing. He showed us the protective, tough-natured side of a correctional officer.

"Then take leave and get," he barked. "It's my job to protect these children, even from you. There's no face-slapping or name-calling in my house. Take me to court if you want to argue about custody, visitation, or support. Game on. I'll work myself to the bone to pay what I got to take care of. But in the meantime, this is their home, and they're not going anywhere. Not on my watch!"

"Dad's in there fixing the toilet. I hope he doesn't find the mashed peas and gravy I flushed last night."

"Why'd you flush your peas a-a-and gravy?"

"They smelled gross."

"Yeah, Mom took a can of peas and s-s-s-stirred in a package of gravy. Not a food connoisseur, but-but-but they didn't go together so good."

"Not like us."

"Yeah," I smiled back, "not like us."

*   *   *

The next morning, Mrs. Napier announced roll, like usual. When she got to "McGee," Alyson cut in, "H-H-Here for all the dummies who can't talk right."

Mrs. Napier stood aghast. Her complexion ripened. Her fingers trembled, and I saw her lips twitch in a way that suggested she wanted to say something but couldn't. Then her sewn mouth continued with, "Eleanor Medfield?"

"Here," Eleanor responded.

That's when I knew. Alyson's mother forged the complaint against Mrs. Napier, rendering the third-year teacher helpless against the dynamics of an attorney with brass wits and a razor-sharp tongue.

Alyson's mom probably caused trouble. If Mrs. Napier is afraid to say anything, it means Alyson has a free pass to make my life miserable.

Alyson's bullying increased threefold. She ridiculed me, mocked me, and made fun of me. Alyson lavished her role as the self-appointed head of the bully brigade. But as she tormented me, badgered me, and made fun of my stutter, little did the two of us know:

1. Sixteen years later, Alyson's husband would join a cult of religious fanatics. They believed they communicated with alien beings through an interpretive goat they snatched from a local ranch.

He ran off with the goat, taking their money and possessions with him, leaving her life in shambles.

2. Her mother couldn't do anything to help; she'd lost her license over a nasty little incident that involved embezzlement.

3. Alyson eventually reached rock bottom and turned to me for help.

4. Me!?!

5. I helped her, even though I knew she would betray me.

6. Several years later, Alyson debuted her bombshell novel *Rolling with a Rock Star: The Truth Behind the Rise and Climb of Mitzy McGee*. It sold 34 copies, netting her a total of $22.00.

16

SILVER CREEKERS

December 1992

Those were the days I spent afternoons riding around the neighbor-hood with Jimmy Jay and the crew. By then, 2-Tall had become too tall in that the fourteen-year-old aspiring guitarist hovered around six-one. 2-Tall had long, spindly legs that reminded me of grasshop-pers, the deepest, chocolatiest eyes, and a mushroom-shaped fro that garnered attention. However, the quality I cherished the most was his personality. 2-Tall was nice.

Chris Lee was a style aficionado. His fashion had a fresh, edgy vibe everyone wanted to emulate. If Chris wore low-cut jeans with shredded knees and bleach stains, the next day, kids at school sported the same attire.

But if there's anyone who jackknifed my heart in a beating frenzy, it was bad Billy Bearheart. Billy's father (a well-respected podiatrist and Native American spokesperson) shared custody every other weekend. Ever since his father started dating the young, dough-brained waitress from Huckleberry's, Billy rebelled in the aftermath of his parent's divorce.

Sometimes, he'd do things like play doorbell ditch. Sometimes, he ditched more than doorbells by skipping out on school. And sometimes, Billy ran off to stay with his grandmother for a couple of days because his parent's drama gave him a case of the rowdies. The more they fought, the more trouble he got in. The sad thing was I had a mad crush on him. He didn't realize it because he was too busy brooding about the circumstances of his life.

Unfortunately for me and my circumstance as Jimmy Jay's little sister and one of the guys, any chance of being more than a sidekick was pure fantasy. So, I rode with them, then hung around the garage as they bantered about one day forming a band. I became the voiceless wallflower as they discussed band names such as Leprosy, Squashing Tomatoes, and Anaphylactic Alleycats. We lived in Silvercreek, so I wasn't surprised when this make-believe band settled on The Silver Creekers.

All the time they talked, planned, and mapped out songs, I sat with my thoughts soaring in daydreams. *Why do I like him? He doesn't even know I exist. He's my brother's friend. I've got to stop admiring his dimples.*

As I pretended to be invisible, Chris Lee, Billy, 2-Tall, and Jimmy Jay laid down the construction for their band. A band that had yet to have their first jam session. A band that formed before Billy knew how to play the drums — or even had a set of drums, for that matter. A band that went through a dozen names and a half-dozen lead singers. A band that took four fourteen-year-old boys from a quiet, unobtrusive neighborhood in Bakersfield, California, and transformed them into rock superstars.

*   *   *

After Christmas, all the ornaments and the pinecone-encrusted wreath were returned to the storage rack atop the rafters. The gardening equipment was relocated to the storage shed at the side of the property while the boxed effects of Sarah McGee lined the sidewall (which

I used as a makeshift bench). Except for Richard's camping equipment, it left a good portion of floor space for us.

I don't remember the exact date; I just remember sitting atop a pile of boxes as Jimmy Jay and 2-Tall stood in the middle of the garage, strumming guitar strings, producing an obnoxious wail that sounded like cats getting run over by an ice cream truck.

I admit inside elements of time and tune their cords meshed for a moment or two. And I could hear they might have been playing the same song. I couldn't tell what song it was or how it should have been played, but I was encouraged by their potential.

Of course, I couldn't see the potential of Billy, whose drum set was a makeshift assortment of pots and pans. Billy assured Jimmy Jay and the rest of us he'd procure a drum set as soon as he could. So, as Jimmy Jay and 2-Tall made a symphony of screaming cats, Billy made a commotion that sounded like a rambunctious three-year-old.

The person no one had to worry about was Chris Lee. Unbeknownst to the rest of us, Chris studied piano since age five. When Chris showed up with a small electrical unit, we thought he'd gone bonkers. Then he played a song, and we all sat, amazed and dumbfounded.

I know stories have gone around that when the band first formed, there was an uproar about Chris taking charge. But there was no turmoil, arguing, trouble, or strife. Chris (the only person who could actually play an instrument) received a unanimous appointment with a smattering of high fives.

So that's it. That's how the band formed. Within a month, the name changed from the Silver Creekers (a poor choice if I say so myself) to the Hamburger Burglars to Whodunits. And even though Billy had yet to procure a drum set from his rich father. Even though Chris patiently explained concepts like rhythm, pitch, tremble, and pause. And even though reading music had hardly become familiar. "Mary Had a Little Lamb" still sounded like a pair of cats getting run over by an ice cream truck — an ice cream truck playing "Mary Had a

Little Lamb," but you get the drift. That's when the crew learned that forming a band took a lot of determination and work.

17

THE RED PEN

January 1993

Richard earned a pretty sweet salary at the prison. Whenever money seemed to run out, he'd work an overtime shift to pick up the slack. Of course, Mom could have worked but chose not to. The day she and Richard tied the knot, she announced her "retirement" from her acclaimed cleaning service, where she actually cleaned a lot more than she should. Richard paid the bills and never complained. He paid my mother's bills and never complained. And he gave her a generous amount (everything left from his paycheck) to take care of the household. Unbeknownst to Richard, my mother spent a hefty portion of that money on herself.

It seemed Mother went to a salon every other day. She had standing appointments at the nail, hair, tanning, and waxing salons. In addition to that, she had weekly appointments with her chiropractor and masseuse. Sometimes, it seemed my mother lived in a make-believe land where Silver Creek was a place for the rich and famous.

And while all this happened, Richard remained in the dark. My doting father didn't notice a disparity in spending because Mother supplemented the household income the same way she always had — by stealing. Mother was an expert at switching tags at department stores. She knew how to have the right outburst at Walmart by insisting items were mispriced. And whenever those strategies didn't work, her greedy fingers stuffed whatever she could in her pockets. I honestly don't know how much she took, but I knew it would be a disaster if Richard found out.

*   *   *

"Mitzy, darling, hop in the car," Mother called as I walked home from school.

Part of me wanted to ignore her; after all, my mother wasn't the type to casually drive along the street, wanting to do something nice. But she was my mother, so I opened the door and slid inside.

"Richard's sleeping off another overtime. Leiann took Marnie to the library. I don't know what the other one's doing, but—"

"Jimmy Jay, M-M-Mother."

Her face scrunched.

"His name's Jimmy Jay. You should start calling him by his name and g-g-g-g-g-get to know him. He's actually a—"

"I thought we'd do some shopping. Doesn't that sound fun?"

"No. Can you drop me off at-at-at the—"

"Geese-Louise, don't be a party pooper! We'll make a few stops, and if you're good, maybe I'll look into getting that skateboard you've--"

"The r-r-r-r-r-red one at—"

"Gosh, your goof-talk hasn't improved. I don't think that stuffy pants, Miss what's-her-name, knows what she's doing."

I shook my head and said nothing. When it came to my mom, I shook my head and said nothing a lot.

"Anyhow, I thought you'd like to know your mother here made finals for a local singing competition." She smiled in a way that suggested she wanted a compliment.

"C-congratulations."

"Everyone's happy for me. You won't believe all the phone calls I've received. I'm so excited. It's for a big-time radio station. If I win, I can move up to county, state, and nationals."

"They have national k-k-k-k-k—"

"Of course, they have national competitions. Many famous people got their start this way. And with my talent and looks, who knows? I could end up a headliner in Vegas."

If she moves to Vegas, she might take us with her!

"Anyhow, I haven't spent a lot of time with you lately, so I thought we'd do a little bonding."

"Okay," I replied.

That's when she said the six words, six terrifying words that signified doom. "First, we'll head to the mall."

My heart cannonballed to my gut.

"It'll be fun!"

As we entered Valley Plaza, my breath stuck. Valley Plaza's the place where she'd been caught shoplifting. As she was stuffed in the backseat of the police car, I stood on the sidewalk, humiliated and disgraced.

"Please don't do anything," I implored. "I-I-I-I don't w-w-want—"

"Mind your mouth," she snapped. "I'm trying to have fun here, and you—"

I stopped at a bench. "C-c-can I just wait here? P-p-p-please?"

"There's this new store I thought we could..."

I wanted to complain that bringing me to the mall to shop for herself wasn't exactly fun, and it sure as heck wasn't bonding, but she grabbed hold of my hand and led me through the door.

"Welcome to Maxine's," the saleslady greeted. "Is there anything, in particular, you're looking for?"

"Just the most spectacular dress!" Engaging salespeople was a part of her ploy. Mother talked the entire time she looked through dresses and while she headed to the plush, sparsely furnished changing room. "I'm new to town, you see, and have a work function. Moved here from Arkansas, where my father has car dealerships and an appliance store. It's my first office social. I'm going to meet the general manager."

"Congratulations," the sales lady replied, "that's awesome."

"This here turquoise one seems puffy an' oversized. Do you have anything smaller?"

"Of course," she responded.

Mother dug into her purse as soon as the lady left, hunting for her handy red pen to alter the price tag.

"Don't," I pleaded, "I-I-I don't—"

The door creaked open. "Sorry, but that's the last one," the sales lady stood empty-handed, "is there anything else I can help you with?"

Mother appeared distraught. She opened her mouth to say something.

"I-I-I-I don't feel so well," I cut her off, clutching my belly. "My stomach doesn't like the-the-the food I ate at school."

"What food?" Mother sighed.

The saleslady's face warmed with concern.

"Sandy Slater's b-b-b-birthday party. I only had five pieces of pizza and a-a-a root beer float." I produced a vulgar, fake belch. "I think I'm gonna be sick."

Mother frowned as the saleswoman practically dove for a waste-basket. "Here you go." She passed it to me. "You poor thing."

And the next thing Mother knew, we were ushered out of the store as if we were lesion-infested carriers of the plague.

"Hurry now," the saleslady pressed, "just a few more steps. Hold the pail close just in case."

Mother said nothing as we crossed the threshold back into the mall thoroughfare.

"Hope you feel better," the saleslady announced. As the door secured, her eyes washed with relief that she wouldn't spend the next hour or so scrubbing pizza and ice cream vomit.

"They don't serve root beer floats in school," Mother grunted as we strode to Ellen's Footwear. But that was it. She didn't yell at me, threaten me, or leave me there. Instead, she dragged me into the next store, where she tried on a dozen pairs of shoes, droning about herself and her aspirations of becoming a karaoke star.

18

BANDANAS

March 1993

I didn't see it when he got up and went to school. I didn't see it when he came home, for that matter, so I'm not exactly sure when it began. But one afternoon at the beginning of March, Jimmy Jay sauntered into the garage, sporting a new fashion accessory. I don't know if he copied it from some rock star on MTV or what, but that's the faze when Jimmy Jay donned bandanas — lots and lots of bandanas.

At the time, his long golden locks flowed halfway down his back. Neighbors gossiped about it while his Sunday school teacher droned her disapproval to anyone who would listen. On the other hand, kids from the neighborhood seemed to take notice, as if long golden hair and a headband gave him street cred. Kids strolled by practice, and our garage became the place to hang out. Pretty soon, Poor Mary no longer sounded like a cat being squashed to a tragic end by that infamous ice cream truck; she actually had a little rhythm and swag.

Then girls showed up, and *all* the guys sported headbands. Billy had one with a skull and crossbones because it fueled his "bad boy" persona. Chris wore whatever coordinated his attire (of course). 2-Tall wore themed bandanas, advertising his allegiance to sports, while Jimmy Jay stuck to a traditional red, white, and blue. Day by day, practice by practice, I remained a quiet, unobtrusive wallflower as I witnessed the miracle of Barfing Stallions unfold.

*   *   *

Once Dad insulated the garage with sound-proofing panels, the guys met at our place almost every afternoon. As soon as the panels went up, Billy Bearheart unpacked his drum set. Therefore, the first official practice for Barfing Stallions happened on a lazy weekend afternoon in March 1993. And the first song (with a lot of help from Chris Lee) sounded like, well, music.

From that day on, the guys stuck to a particular formation. Whether they played on stage at our old high school or the thousands of other venues (*Saturday Night Live*, stadiums, and sports arenas worldwide), they pretty much maintained the same positioning.

Jimmy Jay stood on the right side of the group, where he strummed chords next to the water heater. 2-Tall stood opposite Jimmy Jay by the door opener. And Chris and Billy took over the middle. The side wall, that's where I sat. It's where I lived back then. That's where I nestled amongst Sarah McGee's boxed effects. That's where I listened as they gradually improved. There's one thing, something I realized early on. The guys looked the part. They played the part. They even had a few moves. But one big whopping barrier stood in their way from stardom. None of them could actually sing.

19

LIZZY DAULTON

Mid-May 1993

The first audition for lead vocal went down without a hitch. Jimmy Jay knew a girl from his Algebra class who sang in the school choir. As soon as Elizabeth (Lizzy) Daulton entered the garage, she got the job. Lizzy sang for three and a half practices when her father stormed up the driveway.

"Elizabeth, what are you doing? I thought you were going to the library!"

"Ah," Lizzy's fingers clung to her skirt seam. "Dad, can I stay and practice for—"

"No, of course not! What's gotten into you?"

"Dad, please!"

At that point, we felt bad for her.

"Can I stay? I promise I'll—"

"No way! I'm not allowing you to stay here and hang around these... these..." His gaze spanned 2-Tall, Billy, and Chris Lee. Then his eyes settled on Jimmy Jay (with his wild golden locks and gangster bandana), and his anger exploded.

"Look at them! That boy's hair is long enough to be a, a, a... These boys need haircuts. They need discipline. They need someone to come here with a leather strap and dole out some good old-fashioned respect."

He grabbed hold of Lizzy's forearm.

"Dad, please!?!" She struggled within his restraint.

"I'm gettin' your backside back to our end of the street." He tightened his grasp and proceeded to escort her from the garage. "You're not to speak to them again."

"Don't you think you're being a little hard on her?" 2-Tall cut in, which was strange coming from the kid who did everything he could to avoid conflict. "She wasn't doing anything, only singing. What's wrong with singing?"

Mr. Daulton spun around with a crazed jack-o-lantern expression. Then, for no reason whatsoever, he stormed over to 2-Tall.

"Stand down! Stand down!" Richard's familiar form charged in. "Lay one finger on a minor in *my* garage, on *my* property, in *my* presence, and it'll be a 10-10. I'll go buck wild in his defense."

Mr. Daulton's hand inched towards 2-Tall's throat.

"I said, 'STAND DOWN!' Lay a finger on that kid, and it's GAME ON!"

"I, ah—" Lizzy's father took a step back.

"Sir, you're gonna apologize to this young man." Richard formed a protective shield in front of 2-Tall. "Then, you can get your two-bit self out of *my* garage and off *my* property!"

Mr. Daulton sneered as he spat, "I'm gonna take my daughter and go."

"Kids," Richard decreed, "if any lowlifes bother you, let me know so I can deal with 'em. I don't take kindly to perps who hurt children."

Mr. Daulton ushered Lizzy from the garage.

"And I better not hear you hurt any minors under my care. It's a crime, you know. You lay a finger on a kid, and I'll ensure you get a first-class ticket to the big house. Then it'll be game on. Child abusers are particularly popular on the yard."

Lizzy and her father rushed down the street in frantic footsteps.

"Now what?" Jimmy Jay grumbled.

Richard turned and faced 2-Tall. He panned into the dark caramel eyes of the preteen he'd known since he was a toddler. "Now, we celebrate my man here." Richard wrapped his arm around 2-Tall's shoulder. "Proud of you, son. Like the way you handled yourself."

Everyone came over and slugged or nudged 2-Tall in a display of support. Richard winked at me as we stood in our awkward mob, so I felt included.

"But from now on, no kids are allowed on this property without their parent's permission. You got me?"

"Yes, sir," Jimmy Jay responded.

"Yes, sir," the guys repeated.

"Y-y-y-yes, sir," I said, and everyone spontaneously laughed. I wasn't in the band. I wasn't part of the turmoil. In fact, I said nothing when everything went down. Nevertheless, I stood my ground as a wallflower. For some reason, it made everyone happy. It was the first time my stutter made people chuckle in a good way.

20

VANESSA SANTORINI

Late-May 1993

Ten days later, Vanessa Santorini took reign as lead singer. Vanessa (Leiann's BFF since grade school) aspired to be a famous chef. She offered to fill in only until someone who wanted the aggravation took the job.

Vanessa was kind. That's how we stutterers tend to rate people: by their level of support. If someone insults us right away, they're the people we're wary of. If someone doesn't interrupt (or correct every other word), they're the people we tolerate. And if someone patiently listens to *what* we say instead of the *way* we say it, they're the people we trust. I trusted Vanessa immediately.

"Hey, munchkin," Vanessa greeted. She accompanied Leiann into the kitchen, where they found me at the table in front of a stack of homework.

"H-h-hey."

"You're right," Vanessa said to Leiann. "She's adorable."

"I know." Leiann chuckled. "I got lucky, right?"

"Heck yeah."

"So, what grade are you in?" Vanessa slid into the seat across from me as Leiann retrieved a couple of sodas from the refrigerator.

"F-f-fourth," I ventured.

"Awesome. Who's your teacher?"

"Mrs. Napier."

"She's nice, huh? A little tough but fair. Man-o-man, I bet she's got you doing collaborations. She's like that. I think my brother had to do a hundred of them."

"Yeah," I spouted, "I-I-I-I don't like them. She assigned me to a, a, a group of girls who are kind of mean. It's hard when you-you-you don't like who she sets you up with."

"Heck yeah!" She smiled as Leiann joined us at the table.

I was about to say something else when Marnie crawled into the room on her hands and knees. "I'm *not* Marnie," Marnie announced, "I'm a puppy dog."

Marnie crawled between Leiann and Vanessa and proceeded to shake her imaginary tail. "I'm wagging my tail. I'm not wagging my butt; that would be gross. I'm wagging my cute little tail. I have a cute little tail because I'm a cute little puppy."

"What an adorable puppy," Leiann exclaimed.

"Adorable," Vanessa agreed as she petted Marnie's imaginary fur. "What's your name, little pup?"

Marnie's eyes rolled to the ceiling. "Princess Chocolate Fudge," she announced. "I'm Princess Chocolate Fudge because I like chocolate."

"I'm not sure dogs are supposed to eat chocolate," Leiann chuckled. "I'm pretty sure they—"

"I'm a special kind of dog that eats chocolate."

"Would you like-like s-s-s-some chocolate now?"

"Ruff! Ruff! Ruff ruff ruff. That's 'yes! I'd like some very much!'"

"Geeze, it's a little close to dinner," Leiann fretted. "How about some cereal? I wouldn't want to upset your little girl tummy—"

"Grrrrrrr," Marnie growled.

"I mean, *puppy* tummy."

"Ruff! Ruff! Ruff ruff ruff! You don't have to worry; chocolate's vitamins to my breed."

Leiann retrieved a box of cereal and a bowl.

"If she likes chocolate so much, maybe I'll make some brownies," Vanessa suggested.

I'd like to interject here that I'd never had homemade brownies. I'd had the brownie-like cake from school, from the grocery store (brought by Nana McGee), and the rock-hard monstrosity Mother concocted when she forgot to add eggs. They burnt so badly that the pan's scorched coating stuck to them. Mother told us to pick off the Teflon and eat them anyway. Needless to say, we flushed them down the toilet. *Maybe that's what spawned Marnie's compulsion to flush food.*

"Y-y-y-y-yes!" I spouted.

"Good, I'll bring some tomorrow."

"Can you-you move here? You like to bake, and our mom's not-not-not exactly the best cook. Sometimes her c-c-casseroles look like baby barf."

"Sometimes?" Leiann snickered as she placed the cereal bowl and spoon on the tabletop. "More like—"

"Ruff ruff ruff," Marnie interrupted. "Puppies don't eat cereal from the table. They eat—"

"From the f-f-f-f-floor."

"Yeah, ruff ruff ruff. From the floor."

Leiann and Vanessa looked at each other and shrugged. Without saying anything, Leiann slid the cereal bowl on the clean, tiled floor alongside the baseboard. Marnie crawled over, took the spoon out using her paw (hand), and swiftly discarded it. And then she proceeded to doggy slurp chocolate flakes using her tongue.

"Uh, I'm not sure," Leiann hesitated.

"As long as she's eating, it shouldn't matter," Vanessa decreed. "She needs to grow strong."

Marnie doggy wolfed, "Owwww, chocolatey flakes are a puppy's best friend."

"You're s-s-s-silly, Marnie."

The teenagers laughed. Marnie laughed. And I laughed. We spent the next hour or so just being normal. One of us ate from a doggie bowl and then pretended to poop and pee on the floor, but it was a perfectly ordinary afternoon for my sisters and me.

21

LUELLA FARNSWORTH

June 1993

O nce Vanessa got an A-minus on a report card, she couldn't risk a less-than-stellar GPA. When she stepped down, she recommended her neighbor, Luella, take her place. Luella Farnsworth sang for the next week or so. Luella had attitude. She had spunk. She even knew the songs. Unfortunately, Luella's high notes were so far off that even the walls wept with aggravation.

That's around the time Marnie sported earmuffs. I wasn't sure if Marnie's earmuffs were to prevent inner ear bleeding or if she wanted to prevent her thoughts from being obliterated. I will say wearing snow gear in the middle of mild-mannered Bakersfield did look strange.

Of course, our neighbors weren't happy with Luella's ear-splintering racket. Someone even filed a complaint with the home-owners' association. But as long as practice concluded before 10:00 p.m., Richard remained within the bylaws of his agreement.

Luella (who knew she didn't have the best voice) didn't take kindly to being harassed, so she purchased a small portable microphone. With Luella blasting pitch bombs on the mike and the guys out of sorts with the band, it's a miracle the garage didn't mysteriously incinerate.

Unfortunately, Mother ventured into practice the day before her karaoke competition to put a damper on Luella's dream.

"No, no, no, no, no," Mother snapped. "That's not music, little lady." Mother stepped in front of the microphone. "Let *me* show you how it's done."

"Boys," Mother turned to address the guys, "do you know Tanya Toucher's 'Muddy River'?"

The guys looked baffled. They knew seven songs, including "Mary Had a Little Lamb" and "Mary Had a Little Lamb" rock version.

"Chris, I know you can play it," Mother mused. "You can play anything. Start at the second verse, and I'll join in with an A Minor."

She turned to Luella. "That's a musical note."

Luella's eyes squinted.

Chris froze. He didn't care for my mother. Actually, I don't think anyone there cared for her — well, except Marnie and me. Marnie and I loved her, even though we didn't understand her a lot of the time.

"I suggest you start now unless you want Jimmy what's-his-name in hot water with the homeowner's association."

Mom, don't tell me you're the one who filed the complaint with the Homeowners Association.

"I'll put a stop to these band shenanigans."

Mom, don't! Please go back to the house and let us be.

Marnie walked in with her face covered in so much makeup that she looked like a dunked clown.

"What's going on?" Marnie stood behind Mother. "It doesn't sound like someone's getting smushed under an elephant's butt?"

I gulped. Marnie's face looked bad, really bad. "Marnie, what-what-what-what—"

"Spit it out, for God's sake," Mother snapped. "I don't understand why you can't--"

Mother sensed something was off. She paused, turned, and saw Marnie's face painted in a mosaic of purple, blue, brown, and red splotches. "Is, is, is that *my* makeup?"

"I look like you, Mommy!"

The guys chuckled.

"Why do you act so bizarre?"

The chuckling stopped.

"You're constantly playing around toilets. You act like you're a dog."

"A puppy," Marnie interjected.

"You walk around with headbands and earmuffs and my makeup now!?! This band's ruined my baby. They're turning her into a—"

"Lady," Luella tried to say something.

"MOTHER," I cut in at the top of my lungs, "c-c-c-can I hear you sing?"

It was as if a magic wand drifted through the air and made things right — well, right for my mother.

"Of course," she smiled.

"Lady," Luella tried to speak again.

Chris played a chord, and Mother's voice went a cappella for the opening line of her favorite karaoke number.

"Lady," Luella tried to cut in again.

Mother motioned for Chris to play the accompaniment. Not knowing what else to do, Chris obliged as our mother belted lyrics into the microphone. It was the first time I heard her sing like that. I remember her singing in the car and the shower. I remember her singing as she cleaned people's houses (robbing them blind), but I never really listened. This time, when she sang, I noticed her voice was loud, buoyant, and overly done.

About three verses in, Luella walked over and unplugged the microphone, and then she collected the attachment and stand.

"Bring that back," Mother yelped, "I haven't finished!"

"Lady," Luella finally got to speak her mind, "you're something else. You disrespect the little one in front of her friends. She's your kin; what kind of mama does that?"

Mother gasped.

"You make fun of my gal, Mitzy, here, because she can't talk so good. Heck, I don't know anyone who talks right all the time. We all make mistakes." She gave Mother a stern scowl. "Especially you."

"How dare you," Mother snapped.

"You can't remember your own stepson's name; that's pretty trashy if I do say so myself."

Jimmy Jay looked down.

"You bug, my man Chris, here to play accompaniment for your song. The poor guy is classically trained. You can't hit the right note if a dog bit into your tail end and--"

"Out," Mother growled.

"Oh, I'm leaving, happy to oblige. This, here, microphone's been through enough. I'm gonna take her home and save her from the torment. I'm gonna let her listen to some Billie Holiday, Ella Fitzgerald, and Nina Simone. Heck, I'm even gonna give her a little Dianna Ross."

"What are you talking about?" Mother grumbled.

"Lady, if you don't know what I'm talking about, you have no business impersonating a singer."

Luella spun around and sauntered down the street. "Jimmy Jay," she called before she was out of sight, "see you in class."

"Chris," Mother said as if nothing had happened, "I don't need a microphone. Can you play Patsy Cline's 'Crazed'?"

As I sat imprisoned by my mother's neverending lust to be heard, little did I know how the course of events would affect me. The next day in the library, I checked out books on Billie Holiday, Ella Fitzgerald, Nina Simone, Patsy Cline, and Dianna Ross because that's what geeky girls do. I studied the greats and gained a wealth of knowledge about the legends of music.

Next, I studied other artists and genres, becoming a self-appointed expert on rock, folk, country, jazz, and the blues. After that, I used my beloved books to study the basics of pitch, key, register, and clarity. It may seem nerdy. It may seem like a geeky, dork-headed thing to do, but books were my best friend back then. Sharpening intellects is what we (super-geeks) like to do.

22

THE BEAUFIFUL SARDINE

Mid-June 1993

"How do I look?"

Mother performed a glorious spin, providing Marnie and me the benefit of head-to-toe bling. Her silver sequined dress reflected so much light; it almost had me blinded.

Marnie and I sat at the kitchen table in front of bowls of macaroni and cheese. Jimmy Jay practiced with the band while Richard toiled at the prison, raking in money for household expenses.

"Perfect for a winner, don't you think?"

"Did you say wiener?" Marnie chuckled.

Leiann laughed out loud from the next room.

"No," Mother gasped, "I said, winner. I'm telling you, in this dress, with my talent and looks, I'm expecting my first win."

"N-n-n-nice," I replied. "G-g-g-g—"

"What about my nails." Mother held out her hands, displaying four-inch long, cobalt-blue fingernails. "Do you think they're too showy?"

"Cool," Marnie responded, "like you pasted little dead eel bodies on your hands!"

Leiann laughed a little louder as Mother groaned.

"And in that silver dress, with your hair stuck to your head like that, you look glamorous...."

Mother smiled.

"... like a beautiful sardine!"

"What the..." Mother goaded.

Leiann peeked around the doorway. When she saw Mother's long silver dress, she burst into laughter.

A horn honked from somewhere near the driveway.

"Leiann, make sure they finish their dinner, then send them to bed. Also, I want this mess cleaned and the dishes in the dishwasher put away. When I return, I'm going to want to celebrate and don't want to deal with all this fuss."

Mother started for the door in her slinky stilettos. "Toodles," she quipped before she left.

Once she wiped down the counter, Leiann joined us at the table, where we giggled at the silliness of wiggly eyebrows. We wedged macaroni noodles on our teeth to form fangs. And we made up silly, crazy stories about each other. As usual, we just had fun.

*   *   *

Sometime in the middle of the night, long after we'd drifted to sleep, I heard a rumble of voices from the other side of the stairway.

"What do you mean you forgot?" Mother snapped. "I told you I wanted the dishes from the dishwasher put away. That means I want the dishes put away! You cleaned the countertops, but you didn't finish your chores."

As Leiann mumbled something, I noticed it was two thirty-seven in the morning.

"Whether I won or not doesn't matter. I told you I wanted the dishes put away. That means I want the dishes put away. You didn't take care of your responsibility. Get up and..."

The sound of creaks descended the staircase.

A few minutes later, I heard Leiann ascend the staircase, return to her room, and secure herself inside. Then – as sleep enveloped me in a cocoon of serenity – I awoke to soft seeps of sobbing from a nearby room. To this day, I don't know if it was my mother or Leiann. All I knew was that within the rebounds of laughter and the light-hearted moments of everyday life, there were always nooks and crannies for a good cry.

23

ASHLEY AMOS

August 1993

Tryouts for lead singer occurred six days before school started. By then, the guys could play seven or eight songs; they just needed a singer. So, the group of us set out on our bicycles to cover telephone poles in an assortment of flyers. Each flyer featured a list of qualifications, including parental permission, the ability to read music, work well with others, and a voice.

Shirts had been screen-printed, fingers crossed, hopes edged for a productive turnout. All in all, seven would-be singers ventured up the driveway. Three were overage for a teen band, including Kaylee Desmond's grandma, Chris's Aunt Edna, and this strange person nobody knew named Olé.

Marnie took to Olé immediately. She sat in the lawn chair next to him, fawning over the spider tattoo on his forearm and his long red beard woven into a braid. She tugged on his braid as if it were a magical lamp cord.

Olé (a musician with experience in the military) quickly determined the guys needed a little help. Instead of joining the band,

Olé became a mentor of sorts. As our new mentor assisted with vocal tryouts, Marnie sat on a lawn chair, doodling a spider on her arm.

"Sorry, Todd and Dale," Olé vetted, "but you gotta work on rhythm and tone. If you want to sing for a band, I suggest you consider vocal lessons or, perhaps, you can join a choir. Don't know if it will help. Most singers come by it naturally. Taking lessons and practicing couldn't hurt."

"Thanks," Todd cracked as he took off down the driveway.

"Yeah, thanks," Dale responded, "didn't want to sing with your crummy band anyway."

"Ashley and Simone, that leaves the both of you."

Olé looked over at Jimmy Jay, who nodded in agreement.

"I suggest," Olé addressed the guys, "you have them sing the same song. That way, you can compare voices and see who's the better fit."

The guys nodded in agreement. By then, Marnie had six spiders on her arm.

"Wrong," Ashley cut in. "I'm not singing what she's singing. I brought my own tape."

"What song?" Jimmy Jay asked.

"'Over the Rainbow.' I performed it at school and the Kern County Fair."

"Great," Simone squealed, "I'll sing it also!"

"No, you won't," Ashley huffed. "You can't steal my song!"

"It's not *your* song; it's…"

Marnie finished the army of spiders on her arms and started in on her legs.

Olé turned to my brother. "You're gonna have to learn to deal with this kind of thing. How do you want to proceed?"

"By NOT letting her sing my song!" Ashley snapped.

"By doing the comparison," Simone said smugly.

"They do the same song, like you said," 2-Tall interjected. "We don't want to argue here. This is supposed to be a—"

"Okay, "Ashley gave in, "but she goes after me because it's *my* tape."

"Sounds reasonable," Olé mused. "Guys, what do you think?"

The guys shook their heads in agreement.

As Marnie completed her spider collection on her second leg, the spiders seemed to get scarier. One creepy crawler had gigantic eyes with fangs dripping saliva.

Everyone sat around and expectantly listened while Jimmy Jay inserted the tape into the portable cassette player. As Ashley sang, we sat and politely listened. And I gotta admit, she was pretty good. She hit notes and remained on key for the most part. Once Ashley completed the song, the guys gave her a polite round of applause. I wasn't sure she deserved a round of applause. But she gave me a look, so I felt pressured into clapping.

Next, it was Simone's turn. Simone stood in the same place and started the song in the same way. Unfortunately, as we sat and politely listened, Ashley kept cutting her off.

"Wrong!" Ashley snarled. "She used the wrong word. She said 'a' when it should have been 'the.'" "No, no, no, no, no!" "It doesn't go that way." "She changed the rhythm."

"Shhhhh," Chris cut in, "have some respect."

"YOU have some respect. She's singing my..." Ashley's eyes flared. "Oh, oh, oh, did you hear that? Did you hear that?"

"Wh-wh-wh-wh-what?" I asked, even though I knew I shouldn't have.

"OMG," Ashley scoffed, "what's wrong with her? Is that a stutter? God, I hope she's not with the band. I don't know if I can sing with a band that has a—"

"Can you stop?" Simone paused. "I'm singing here, and you—" Simone regarded the guys and realized they had a lot of growing up to do before they could handle the discord of managing a singer. She silently collected her backpack and left.

"I guess I'm it," Ashley cheered triumphantly. "I'm the new lead singer of... Um, what's the band's name again?"

"She's An Airhead," Marnie quipped. By then, Marnie's arms, legs, and neck featured an elegant medley of spiders and a scared-looking fly that was about to get eaten.

Olé mentored the band when he had time. Unfortunately, a few months later, Olé succumbed to depression and dropped out of sight. We searched for him for years; it became aggravating. Everyone was worried. We even wrote a song about stress and PTSD. Fortunately, years later, Marnie found him at... Hum, well, I guess you'll have to wait to get to that part. I don't want to ruin the surprise.

24

CODE III

October 1993

Richard walked in from the night shift and found me hunched over the breakfast table in a mild state of panic.

"Your new glasses look good, really good. They make you look even more beautiful — if that's possible."

Mother nodded in agreement as she set down a basket of bagels.

"I wish I saw blurry," Marnie declared, "so I could get glasses like Mitzy."

"Tinted lenses," Jimmy Jay added. "Next time, get them tinted so your teacher can't tell if you're sleeping."

As breakfast continued, Richard lectured that sleeping in class wasn't up to conduct. Jimmy Jay wolfed down his food and had seconds. And then Mother discovered Marnie didn't comb the hair clump on the back of her head. Minutes later, I shuffled out the door for a typical day of hibernating in the library, pretending I didn't exist.

*   *   *

That afternoon - as I sat in the garage amongst Sarah McGee's effects, completing my homework - I tried my best to ignore any drama.

"Seriously, as lead singer and star, I should have a say in this." Ashley flipped her hair. "And I say we venture into folk music."

"What?" Jimmy Jay grunted. "That's not what my friends want to hear."

"I don't care what your friends want to hear. I want to play what *I* like."

"Then you should play songs that sound like wolves tearing into baby animals," Marnie vetted. "Because that's what you--"

Marnie didn't look well. Her hair looked messy like it usually did. Her face looked smooshed like it usually did. However, something about her complexion seemed off.

"Why does *she* have to be here?" Ashely snapped. "In fact, why does either of them have to be here? They're not in the band. They don't help with anything, and they're weird. They just get in the way. I don't understand why your freak little sisters are here. Why do I have to put up with--"

Marnie suddenly collapsed onto the floor. Jimmy Jay and the guys rushed over to render aid as I ran in and got Dad.

"Daddy! D-D-D-Daddy! Get up! Th-there's an emergency with-with-with Marnie. In the garage!"

"What happened?" He flew out of bed in his tee shirt and sweats.

"I-I-I don't know. She-she…"

"She's breathing," Jimmy Jay fretted, "but she's unconscious and won't wake up."

"There's no time," Richard barked as he scooped Marnie into his lean, steely arms. "An ambulance can take up to fifteen minutes. Not gonna play around with chances like that when the hospital's just a short bit away. Gonna rush her there, Code III."

We froze as overwhelmed statues.

"Leiann, get my phone on the charger. Jimmy Jay, truck's open. You and 2-Tall slide in the back and buckle her in."

Seventeen seconds later, Marnie awoke as she sat strapped between Jimmy Jay and 2-Tall.

"Dad, here's your phone," Leiann spouted.

"Good, we're gone," Richard announced as he closed the door. Through the open window, he relayed, "Call Mercy Southwest. Tell them to expect us. Then call your mom and—"

But it was too late. His tires squealed as they sped off down the street.

* * *

"What about practice?" Ashley whined. "We can still go on without..."

Never did I want to clobber anyone as much as I wanted to clobber Ashley that day. It took all my strength and willpower not to punch her in the chin or bust a kneecap.

"Man," Chris shook his head as he packed his equipment, "Marnie's right: you are like a rabid wolf. I can see you tearing into—"

And even though the situation was dire, I snickered because I thought what Chris said was funny.

"Shut up, freak face," Ashley snapped. "You can't speak right. You can't talk right. You can't do anything—"

"S-S-S-Speaking and-and talking are the same thing."

"See," she decreed with a snooty sneer. "See what I mean. You don't belong here. You don't belong out here with us cool kids. You're a freak. You're a freak who wears glasses and can't talk. You're a freak from a loser mom who will always be a loser!"

I don't know if it was the stress of the situation. My worry for my sister. My embarrassment at being called names in front of Billy Bearheart (whom I still had a mad-crazy crush on). Or my insecurities in that I inwardly believed some of what she said was true. But I did something horrible that day, worse than clobbering her or kicking her in the knee. Instead of speaking up for myself (and my mom), I fell to the floor and burst into tears. I cried like a wounded animal, with so much snot and guttural wails that I embarrassed myself. Then I wailed even louder.

"Gosh," Ashley grumbled as she gathered her belongings, "I didn't know the little dweeb had that much in her."

* * *

Mother showed up twenty minutes later. We loaded into her car and headed to the hospital.

"What'd you do?" Mom snapped at Leiann. "I was only gone for forty minutes and—"

"You were gone for a lot longer than that."

"Don't speak to me with that tone. I was only gone for a bit. Now I wanna know what happened. What did you do to my beautiful baby?"

"Your beautiful what? I barely seen you spend five minutes with her. I—"

"I'm tired of your accusations. I run a good home, and all you do is—"

"M-M-M-Mom," I attempted to intervene.

"If you were at the house, you'd—"

"Stop!" I cut in. "Please, no f-f-f-fighting. Marnie passed out. Dad took her to the hospital. Leiann had n-n-n-n--"

"Quiet," Mother snapped. "I gotta focus on the road."

As I stressed and stewed about Marnie, Leiann grasped my hand. "Don't worry," she whispered so Mother wouldn't hear. "I'm sure everything will be okay."

When we arrived at the emergency room, Leiann and I rushed inside. Mother's heels made a crude clacking as she followed behind.

"Richard!" Mother squealed when he stepped from behind an open door. "I'm here. I'm here. I made it."

"Good," he replied calmly, "but prepare yourselves."

"What!?!" Mother gasped. Her hand dramatically flew to her forehead.

"Not now, Vicki. Be calm."

"What should we prepare for?" Leiann looked terrified.

"Dad, I'm-I'm-I'm scared."

"This's the time," his voice soothed, "we gotta stick together as family."

"W-W-W-Why, Daddy?"

"Because," he leaned over till we were eye-to-eye, "the doctor suspects something might be wrong with her heart."

* * *

"Hey," Marnie greeted from her bed. "I'm in a hospital. It's my first time. Well, except for when I was born, but I don't remember that. Look, look, look, I gotta real hospital bracelet. And see this cute gown. It's a hospital gown. It has kittens on it. Isn't it—"

"Marnie," I screeched as I rushed over. "I-I-I-I—"

"I was worried about you, baby," Mother cut in. "How are you doing? Are they taking good care of you?"

"Yeah, except for this IV. I couldn't feel it when they pricked me, but I know it must of hurt."

Leiann and Jimmy Jay settled into the chairs next to Marnie's bed as Mother continued with her questions. "Did they say what's wrong? How long have you been here? Where's your doctor? I'd like to know what's going on."

"Victoria," Richard cut in, "the doctor will be here in a few—"

The door opened, and a tall Korean-American woman walked in wearing hospital scrubs.

"Are-are you my-my sister's—"

"Doctor," Mother cut in, "where've you been? I'm worried sick about my little girl. Can you tell me what's going on? What's happened? How long will she be here?"

Jimmy Jay and Leiann remained an oasis of praying eyes and knotted fingers.

"Hello, Mr. and Mrs. McGee," Dr. Kim greeted. "Hello, Miss Marnie." She reached down and patted my sister's forearm. "I'm a pediatric cardiologist – that's a heart doctor – who just happened to be checking on a patient when Dr. Howard asked me to stop by."

"What is it?" Mother cut in. "What do you—"

"Victoria." Dad wrapped his arm around her shoulders.

In that split-second, I saw how much she depended on him. I saw how he soothed her nerves, putting to bay the storm that brewed beneath her plastic exterior.

"I'm gonna take a little listen," Dr. Kim announced, "before I make an initial diagnosis."

When Dr. Kim placed her stethoscope on my sister's chest, Marnie's face beamed with a ginormous smile.

"Can you hear it?" Marnie gushed. "Can you? Huh? Huh?"

Dr. Kim raised her head. "What?"

"All the love," Marnie vetted. "If you're listening to my heart, you can hear a buttload of love."

"Oh, my," Mother gasped, embarrassed.

Dr. Kim chuckled. "Just be still for a few more seconds."

The room swallowed in silence.

Boom, boom, boom, my heart thundered.

"Ahh, yes."

"Well," Jimmy Jay asked. "What'd you hear?"

Dr. Kim adjusted her stethoscope as she regained her posture. "There's so much love in that great big heart of hers; it might have formed an itty-bitty hole."

"What?" Mother went pale as she grabbed hold of the bedrail.

"Like a flat tire?" Marnie squealed. "I have a flat tire in my chest." For some reason, Marnie found this amusing.

"Dr." Richard cut in, "what does this mean?"

"Could be nothing." Dr. Kim went to the basin and washed her hands. "Something like this might resolve with time. She could grow out of it. I may prescribe some medication, just in case. Or it may mean a short hospital stay sometime in the future, maybe a stitch or two, nothing complicated. We have less invasive procedures to fix this sort of thing. We'll keep her for now and run a few tests. If her vitals remain stable, and she continues to look good, she'll be discharged in the morning."

"Thank goodness," Mother huffed.

"How," Leiann cut in. "How did something like this happen?"

"Oh, it could be a lot of things, but I suspect it's something she may have been born with."

"Something she was born with?" Leiann puzzled. "How? Why are babies born with—"

"It's far too early to speculate." Dr. Kim stuffed her hands in her pockets. "I've read studies indicating various factors. Some indicate it's genetic. Other's that it's an environmental factor during pregnancy."

"What does that mean?" Leiann shook her head.

"What drugs were prescribed? If the mother smoked during her pregnancy. If she was exposed to..."

Time spun as the walls closed in on me. Everything the doctor said, Leiann said, and Marnie's happy pigtails drifted around the room like haunted Christmas decorations.

Mother, YOU did this. YOU smoked during your pregnancy.

"And I can have macaroni and cheese and carrot cake?"

"Yes," Dr. Kim assured. "Once we've conducted the tests, you can eat all the cake you want... but I'd prefer you'd have some of our meatloaf or Jell-O. Our cook makes the best gelatin in the world."

"Yippy," Marnie squealed, "I can't wait!"

* * *

Marnie needed to urinate in a bowl and take tests, so Jimmy Jay, Leiann, and I reported to the visitors' waiting room. As soon as we arrived at the carpeted oasis, I noticed something remarkable. First, it was two, then four, but within twenty to thirty minutes, there must have been a dozen of Richard's correctional coworkers. Most sported uniforms. A few sported civilian attire, while one woman wore a polyester blue business suit as if she managed a luxury hotel.

"Brought you, kids, some pizza," the woman greeted.

"Thanks," Jimmy Jay relayed. "Who are you?"

"I'm Warden Honeycutt," she announced with a twinkle in her eye. "We've come to offer support. We also brought some bottled water. I bet you, kids, are thirsty."

"Yes, thank you so much," Leiann replied. "Thanks for every-thing."

Mother and Richard strolled into the waiting room, holding hands. When Warden Honeycutt and the officers saw Richard, they immediately rose from their chairs. One by one, they approached Richard and offered kindness and compassion.

Mother looked surprised initially but spent the next hour or so conversing with a red-bearded officer with blazing eyebrows. As she entertained Red Beard with stories about her father being the town sheriff and escapades at the family horse ranch, my brain swarmed.

Mother, you did this. YOU. DID. THIS.

*   *   *

Mom and Dad wanted us (kids) to go home, but we declined. So, we spent the night on the visitors' benches, surrounded by blue walls and a parade of prison employees toting cookies and kindness.

Fortunately, Marnie's test results showed only a pin-point hole, which Dr. Kim indicated should heal with medication. Marnie was discharged a little after nine.

"I getta ride in a wheelchair," she squealed as we headed to the parking lot. "Never rode in a wheelchair before. This is fun!"

Marnie held up the bag that contained her brand-new Polypropylene washbasin.

"This's awesome!"

25

FIVE MONTHS LATER

March 1994

I
t happened the second I entered the garage. I'd gone there to
summon Marnie to the kitchen when I caught sight of something
so horrendous it felt like an arrow piercing my heart. That arrow
triggered a course of events that forever changed me.

Ashley stood by the drums, conversing with Billy Bearheart.
That's what got me. That's what impaled my heart. Ashely batted her
lashes while her lips pouted. And she had the audacity to giggle as she
tucked a lock of hair behind her ear. The monster was flirting!!!

No, no, no, no, no! my thoughts fisted. *Stay away from Billy Bearheart. That's my crush! You can't have the most gorgeous boy in the world,
with long dark hair, smoldering eyes, and the cutest smile imaginable. He
doesn't know it yet, but he's mine!*

"Oh, drat," Ashley moaned when she saw me. "Looks like the
nerdy nuisance is gonna pester us again."

Billy gave her a stern scowl.

"Watch it, Ash," Jimmy Jay growled. "That's my sister. What'd
I tell you?"

"I know. I know. It's just infuriating--"

100

"Marnie," I cut in, "come in-in-in-inside to t-t-t-t-take your pills."

Marnie rose from her little pink chair. As she headed towards the access door, she paused before Ashley. "Ashley Anus," Marnie taunted, "I just—"

"*AMOS!*" Ashley screeched. "My last name is AMOS! How many times do I have to tell you?"

"Right," Marnie beamed. "A-NUS. Anyhow, you have a huge booger in your nostril. I think it got tangled in all that nose hair. Man," Marnie squinted as she peered in Ashley's nose, "you have a whole forest in there."

"Get!" Ashley snapped. "Go take your medicine so you don't fall out or die or anything."

"Watch it," Jimmy Jay growled again. "I warned you that I'm tired of how you treat my sisters."

"They're not really your—"

"Say it!" Jimmy Jay challenged. "Say one more thing, and we're done."

"What are you gonna do?" Ashley gloated. "You need me. I'm the star. I'm the lead singer. Heck, Turtle Poopers would be nothing without me."

"Okay, okay," 2-Tall cut in, "everyone chill. We're a band. That means we're family. We gotta stick together and stop acting like—"

"No," Ashley scorned, "I'm not going to candy-coat it anymore. She's a freak. That little girl is a freak!" She pointed at me. "She's a loser. Heck, I doubt she can do anything right."

Jimmy Jay stormed over to Ashley, but the guys cut him off.

"I-I-I-I can-can…" I don't know why I spoke up for myself. Usually, I just let her lambast me with insults. This time, however, I just caught her flirting with Billy Bearheart. "…tell you a-about m-m-m-music."

"What, YOU?" Ashley smirked, pleased with herself.

"That-that-that-that—"

I wanted to explain what I learned. I wanted to explain enunciation, clarity, pitch, and key. Unfortunately, my speech disorder got the best of me.

"That-that-that-that-that--"

"Here," Ashley taunted as she passed me the microphone. But this time, instead of insulting my intelligence or calling me names, Ashley conceived a new, crueler way to belittle me. "Prove it. Prove you know whatever it is you want to tell me. Sing. Sing part of any song, and I'll stop. I'll stop calling you a stupid freak and all the other names."

As I grasped the microphone in my trembling hand, Ashley gloated. Her squeaky-clean shoes practically skipped in place as she awaited my ruin. Ashley walked over to Marnie's chair, settled into the seat, and crossed her legs, donning a triumphant smirk. "I'm waiting," she chanted.

All eyes were on me. Jimmy Jay looked like a wounded bear. 2-Tall, Chris, and Billy stood motionless and visibly distraught. For some reason, they must have known this was the end of Turtle Poopers.

What can I lose? They already think I'm a loser and a freak. They've heard me stutter the simplest words. It can't be any worse than the hundreds of times I messed up the band's name, their names, even my own family's name.

With reserved reluctance and a wearied hand, I raised the microphone. I paused for a second or two of brain-numbing silence. And then I whispered the first few notes of "Somewhere Over the Rainbow" without flaw.

Ashley's gloat began to wane when I went on to sing the fourth, fifth, and sixth notes on key without faltering. I continued singing louder and with feeling as my confidence grew. Halfway through the song, I felt an incredible rush of freedom.

I can sing! I can sing! I can sing!!!

I completed the song and realized my voice didn't falter, stammer, or pause. Not once! I made every note, key, and syllable using the voice in my head. And I realized the singing part of my brain overrode the stuttering part of my brain. I could sing! I could sing without flaw!

The moment I completed the song, the guys rushed over.

"Mitz," Jimmy Jay roared as he hoisted me in the air, "THAT was awesome! You're good! Really, really, really good! A thousand times better than anyone we've had!"

"Really awesome," the guys decreed. "You've got talent!" "I can't believe it!" "All this time, you could sing like that?" "Shoot, we had our lead singer under our noses, and nobody knew."

As the guys celebrated, Ashley got up, hoisted Marnie's pink chair over her head, and smashed it onto the ground.

"You can't fire me," Ashley spat as she stormed down the driveway, "'cause I already quit!"

And that, ladies and gentlemen, is how eleven years old me became the lead singer for Inside-Out Raviolis — or was it still Turtle Poopers at the time? Either way, that's how a stuttering misfit kid like me got the privilege of joining the band. The first step on our road to fame: becoming teenagers!

SECTION III

AGES ELEVEN TO FOURTEEN

26

CHOCOLATE-PIMPLED RUT

May 1994

The day Ashly forced the audition, I belted out lyrics without stuttering, passing out, or barfing all over myself. And it felt good — really good. I knew then and there it would be a significant change in my life. It marked the transition from being a regular freak geek to some sort of super geek. This girl could sing!

But, hey, whoa, I soon realized there's a lot more to singing than blowing notes; after all, that's basically what my mother did. As a singer, I was like a toddler who'd taken her first step but still needed to master climbing on a chair, sliding off a chair, and then dragging the chair across the room without face-planting on the floor.

If that wasn't bad enough, my nerves started to get at me. My stupid, stupid nerves gave me a case of the jitters, even in front of the crew. I don't know if I'd call it stage fright (a beast I'll discuss later) because we were in the garage. But every time we practiced, I experienced uneasiness. Bad report card uneasiness. Ruining Mother's silk top and hearing her frantically searching for it -- yeah, that kind of uneasiness.

So even though the guys were supportive, singing came with a lot of bellyaches and burnt feelings. For a girl who stuttered my entire life – who wanted nothing more than to hide in the library – I honestly didn't know what I'd gotten into. And, slowly but surely, I sank into this thick, invisible stew of disappointment.

The guys were a different story. Day by day, Grape Jelly Dinosaur improved. They synchronized beats. They learned new songs. And they encouraged one another. They did this because they had a lot of encouragement -- the girls. Hordes of different-sized, shaped, and sandaled teenagers strolled by the open garage door. After a while, it got labeled "the pretty parade."

Jimmy Jay and 2-Tall practiced day in and day out; they even took guitar lessons. Looking back on that year, I can't recall seeing Jimmy Jay without his guitar. Heck, I even caught him leaving the bathroom with it strapped on his shoulder. Hate to think of what he was doing with it in there (or the unhygienic implications); I'm just letting you know how seriously my brother took the band.

Billy Bearheart, on the other hand, seemed to absorb talent naturally. He watched music videos and learned by mimicking famous drummers. I know, I know, weird — huh? But that's the honest-to-goodness way he acquired his skill. He watched and copied again and again until he was good.

Chris already knew how to play the piano. What he perfected was the know-how to manage a band, which started with documentaries — a lot of documentaries. Within a year, Chris became a self-appointed expert on the rise and fall of famous musicians. Unfortunately, after reading articles on other groups' self-destructions, Chris made his first rule — a horrible, horrible, horrible rule! The worst rule imaginable: *No Dating Within the Band.* That meant as long as Grape Jelly Dinosaur (or whatever we were) was in existence, I couldn't, shouldn't, wouldn't date Billy. *Nooooooo!*

Ninety-five percent of my reason for being there was Billy. Billy was my inspiration for getting out of bed, brushing my teeth, and getting dressed in something half-decent. I had this mad-crazy crush on this gorgeous Native American god of a teenager, and I'd never be able to carry out my desire to hold his hand or have that inevitable, ever-perfect first kiss.

I knew Chris's rule made sense. Plagues of broken relationships marked the downfall of many good bands. Chris was just looking out for us. He set the foundation that made us great. But, still, denying my heart's desire had me wallowing in a vat of dreariness. And fudge — lots and lots of fudge.

Yeah, sorry to say, I drowned my sadness in junk food nirvana. Donuts, cookies, potato chips, chocolate — I loved them all. Unfortunately, I loved them so much that I began to get puffy. That's nothing compared to what happened to my face. Large, radiant pimples plastered my skin in a garden of acne. *NOOOO!* As if having a stutter wasn't bad enough, by the time I reached thirteen, I was zit-faced and plump.

Therefore, the biggest thing that stood in my way was... me. I couldn't get past my insecurities. Don't get me wrong, I could sing, but I lacked authenticity. I lacked the know-how. And I definitely lacked passion. As the guys went to their lessons, gained expertise, and improved – I sank into a songbird's worst place. I was in a rut.

27

EXAM ROOM 6

June 1994

The blowout between Mother and Leiann happened on the last day of school. Leiann left two days later. I can't put into words how much it shattered my heart. Life didn't feel the same without her goodness, guidance, and macaroni and cheese. I secretly wouldn't have minded if it was the other way around (Mother left while Leiann stayed), but that would have altered the course of our journey. As I look back on it, I appreciate fate's terrible twist of events because the outcome for all of us wouldn't have been quite the same.

With Leiann gone, Mother started going out less. She assumed part of the responsibility of being a mother figure, while Leiann -- well, fate led her down some remarkable paths. Of course, I didn't know about that then. All I knew was I missed my sister with this guttural sadness that cursed every breath. The only stable thing in my life back then – the thing I awoke to every morning and kept my heart homed – was Sarah McGee's mural. Waking up in that enchanted room felt like an oasis of love. I felt protected from all the bad things in the world. I felt safe.

* * *

June 24th tested that sense of safety and security.

"Girls!!!" Mother called from the hallway. "Get up; there's an emergency! Get dressed and out to the car! We're leaving!"

Now, I didn't know if she'd gotten into another argument with Richard (they had a six-day separation/fallout when Mother got arrested for shoplifting). And I didn't know if Nana McGee had another cat scare. Heck, I didn't know if an ax-wielding intruder broke into the house, and we had to make a quick getaway. All I knew was that as Marnie and I fumbled to get dressed, we heard Mother bellow from the next room. "Johnny, quick, get out of bed!"

Jimmy Jay, Mother. Not Johnny. Not Bobby. Not Tony. And certainly not Steve. Jimmy! Jimmy! Jimmy! Jimmy!

"Hurry and get to the car. We're leaving!"

Four minutes later, Jimmy Jay and Marnie belted themselves into the back seat of Mom's SUV while I sank into the passenger seat next to Mom.

"Mama, what is it?" Marnie looked worried. "Is Nana okay?"

"What's going on?" Jimmy Jay asked.

"What's h-h-h-happening?"

"Listen..." As Mother clutched the steering wheel, I realized her hair wasn't done, she had no makeup, and she wasn't drenched in her regular vat of perfume. In fact, it's the first time Victoria McGee ever left a house in slippers.

"Something happened at the prison."

"DADDY!" Marnie screeched.

"W-w-wha—"

"Is my dad okay?" Jimmy Jay's voice cracked.

"I don't know. Some secretary-person called and told me they had him at San Joaquin Valley Hospital."

Marnie's chin trembled as tears burst from her eyes. I still tried to get the word *what* out while Jimmy Jay's eyes pitted with worry... and dread.

Mother turned onto Ming Avenue. "Something about a distur-
bance in a nearby dorm and people getting shot or stabbed."

"DADDY!" Marnie screeched louder.

I looked back and saw Jimmy Jay's complexion sicken to a stew of
ghastly grays. I didn't say anything at the time, but I knew San Joaquin
was where his mother died.

No one said anything for the remainder of the trip. We were all
too scared to voice our fears. As soon as we pulled into the parking lot
at the emergency entrance, Jimmy Jay took off in a dead run toward the
hydraulic doors. Marnie followed Jimmy Jay. Mother and I followed
Marnie.

* * *

The waiting area of the emergency department was wall-to-wall
prison people. Four stone-faced officers stood guard over a prisoner
in a bright orange jumpsuit. The prisoner had chains around his torso,
bandages wrapping both hands, and an ugly gash on his face that oozed
blood. When he saw us rush in, he smiled, displaying a ghoulish parade
of coffee-brown teeth.

"Get Zepeda outta here!" an officer shouted. "Got kids showing
up. Take him to the back and get him secured."

"You're here," greeted the massively statured, red-bearded guy
with blazing eyebrows (the one Mother befriended at Mercy Southwest.) Since his uniform had a nametag, I learned his name was
Barney.

As Barney ushered us to the side of the room, I noticed Warden
Honeycutt with several official-looking people. They sat still as statues
while the room swarmed with officers, patients, and staff.

"Where's Richard!?!" Mother practically screeched.

"No need to panic," Barney soothed. "Your husband's okay. He
got a few stitches. He'll—"

"WHAT HAPPENED?" Jimmy Jay snapped.

"When McGee... Ah, I mean, when your father returned to his
dorm from submitting his count slip, he noticed unusual movement
in the windows of the building next door. He called it over the radio

and ran over to help. That's when he found two fellow officers being assaulted by a dozen prisoners."

Barney glanced towards Inmate Zepeda.

"Why's HE still here?" he snapped at the officers. "Got family here. Take him to the back. NOW!"

"Where's my dad?" Jimmy Jay stood visibly shaken. "I wanna see him."

"In Exam Room 6," Barney said in a hushed tone, "but before you go, you gotta know something."

"What?" Mother asked skeptically.

"Tonight, Slick Rick... ah, I mean Officer McGee, jeopardized his safety by saving the lives of two officers."

"Okay," Mother started and then stopped.

"Eleven inmates bum-rushed the office, ambushing Acosta and Meyers with substantial beat-downs. Ah, I mean, injuries. Acosta's in surgery. He'll live, but they suspect he might have a half dozen broken ribs, a cracked orbital socket, and a shattered jaw. Meyers got stuck six times with an inmate-manufactured shank. We suspect it's the same one they used on your husband."

Mother gasped.

"Don't worry; they only got your husband in the back, nothing life-threatening."

"When can I see him?"

"Just one thing. Every second counts when you're gettin' beat like that. If McGee hadn't rushed in and gone buck wild saving them people like he did, I got no doubt we'd be scooping two of our own in body bags. McGee saved their lives. He's a fricken' legend."

"O-O-O-Okay," I muttered. My heart swelled with pride.

"Came here to tell you this 'cause I suspect Warden Honeycutt and her crew of backstabbers ain't here for the right reason. McGee broke code. He should have waited for backup."

"Are you saying my husband is in hot water because he shouldn't have saved their lives? That he should have stood there like a dimwit and just watched those people get beaten and bludgeoned to death?"

Mother looked over at Warden Honeycutt and produced her grandest fake smile.

"Exactly," Barney urged in a hushed tone. "They won't let me back there, but I need to give McGee a message. Tell him I've got his back. I called in the cavalry. Got a union rep on her way right now. Tell him--"

"No need." Mother waved dismissively. And then she passed Barney and all of the staff members, administrators, and inmates as her tall, svelte, grubbily dressed form led us (kids) down the hall to Richard's room.

* * *

"D-D-D-D-Daddy," I cried as Marnie spouted, "Daddy! Daddy! Daddy!"

Jimmy Jay rushed to his father's side. "Dad, are you okay?" He grasped the rail of the gurney. "We heard there was a fight. What happened? Are you okay?"

Richard chuckled as he reached over and one arm hugged each of us. "I'm fine. I'm fine."

He tilted his head and winked at Mother.

"No need to worry. Just got poked. No big deal," he chuckled.

When I saw my dad laugh like that, an elephant of uneasiness evaporated from the room.

"Yay," Marnie cheered. Her eyes lit as she hopped on her tiptoes. "Since we're here, maybe we can get some gelatin."

"Sounds like the perfect plan, kiddo," Richard smile scrunched. "Couldn't have masterminded a better idea myself."

"Dad, I was worried," Jimmy Jay's voice cracked. "They say you—"

"Now-now-now, I don't want you fretting none. I'm fine, I promise. I'm fine. I've never lied to you before, so I don't want no sourpuss faces or sadness."

His eyes tenderly locked in on Mother's. She smiled and nodded in acknowledgment.

"You can stay for a few minutes, and then I'll get Barney or one of the crew to take you home for a 10-10 so you can have a good night's rest. Your mom needs to stay to get me out of here once the doc signs my discharge."

He glanced towards Mother. "Okay, Dear?"

Mother nodded in return, then stepped out of the room to ask for some gelatin.

"Dad, I wanna stay," Jimmy Jay pleaded.

"Right here ain't a hundred percent safe."

I wasn't sure if Richard meant the presence of inmates or the administrators.

"All I care about is my family. I want you, kids, back home where you're safe in bed, getting a good night's rest."

Ten minutes passed, and a nurse entered the room with a packaged dessert tray. She passed one to each of us kids and put two on the tray table, presumably for Richard and my mom.

"Thanks, Ling," Dad called to her, "you're the best."

* * *

I sat on one side of Richard while Marnie and Jimmy Jay sat on the other, enjoying strawberry gelatin deliciousness. As crazy as it seems, we were having a good time. Here we sat in a curtained nook in the emergency room – with a cyclone of chaos and shouting all around (including inmates and their scary tattoos) – as we chatted, chuckled, and shared joy. Then the curtain whipped aside, and Warden Honeycutt and two staunchly-postured administrators obstructed the threshold.

"Officer McGee," Warden Honeycutt announced, "family time's over. We'd like a word with you. We have concerns about your flagrant disrespect of protocol."

Richard tried to act as if he wasn't alarmed. "We're just finishing up," his voice cracked. "They'll be on their way shortly."

"Oh, *heck* yeah," Mother snickered as she awkwardly squeezed past them to return to the room. In her grubby clothes with hair half brushed and half all over the place, she resembled a madwoman. "It's about time you got your stuffy pants in here and congratulated this here husband of mine for saving the lives of his fellow officers. Is this a two-bit show or what?"

Jimmy Jay gasped as my mind imploded.

Mother, DON'T. Not now. You don't always have to be the center of attention!

Warden Honeycutt's perfectly drawn brows about skidded off her face. Her administrators stood stunned.

"Vicki," Richard attempted to stop her in his mildest tone. "Vicki, please, I—"

"Yes, Mrs. McGee," Warden Honeycutt coaxed with a hint of snake, "Do. Go. On."

"Instead of supporting your staff. Instead of being with the officers who got hurt, you're sitting out there in your cheap knockoff suit, scheming ways to stab people in the back. That's pretty fricken' trashy if I do say so myself." Mother had globs of makeup under her eyes. Her sweatshirt had a merlot stain on her right boob, while the top snap of her jeans had come undone.

No, Mother, NO! NO! NO! NO! What are you doing? You'll ruin Richard's career!

"You're gonna tell *ME* what's trashy," Warden Honeycutt scoffed.

The administrators gloated as they nudged each other.

"Yeah," Mother gibed, "me and Lou Greenshield."

Warden Honeycutt's smirk melted as an uncomfortable silence descended over the room.

Who's Lou Greenshield?

"Excuse me," Warden Honeycutt snapped. "Who did you say?"

"You heard me. Lou Greenshield. Attorney General Lou Greenshield, the guy in charge of all the prisons for the state. You know, your bosses' bosses' boss. Did I say that right? Is there another 'boss' in there? I can't be sure."

No one said anything.

"Heck, yeah. By the way, he thinks what you're doing here is pretty scummy. Wouldn't be surprised if the director of corrections, himself, didn't call and give you a good ear yanking about this, here, shady business."

Oh, no, Mother. Please don't spout another story about your father. Is this another lie?

"I don't believe you," Warden Honeycutt decreed.

Almost immediately, a pager chirped. The room fell into a trance as Warden Honeycutt retrieved the pager from her jacket pocket and viewed the number on the screen.

"There's no way," she fumed with agitation, "someone like you can be—"

And then Mother said three little words that sent several people's lives into tailspins.

Those three words cast Warden Honeycutt and the administrators from the room. The next day, Richard received a fancy houseplant and three months off on paid family leave. Five months later, he was awarded a meritorious service and heroism medal.

Those three words (although meant to help Richard) exposed a lie that added an invisible layer of rifts to their already threaded marriage. And those three words forever changed my life.

Mother walked across the room till she stood behind me. She delicately put her hands on my shoulders. And then – out of the blue – she made the most fantastical statement I'd ever heard. "He's Mitzy's grandfather."

28

GALAXY OF GOOFINESS

August 1994

R ichard was home for three months, and for us (kids), it was pretty fricking amazing. Richard took us to the beach, the mountains, the movies, and the zoo. Richard made dinner each night. And Richard (seeing my tendency to spend a little too much time huddled inside books) encouraged outdoor activities — lots of outdoor activities.

Richard taught Marnie and me how to roller-skate, skateboard, play tennis, and fish, and he took us on walks each evening as he pointed out stars. Of course, Marnie and I knew Richard made up half the names unless there really is a "Chocolate Cupcake Constellation" that feeds the "Galaxy of Gargoyle Goofiness" or a star called "Princess Poutiness." It was just fun to listen to Richard's crazy banter.

One thing about Richard: he took exercise seriously, but he never browbeat or forced anything. He just made walking, swimming, and miniature golfing fun. Never had I felt so alive. I'm somewhat ashamed to admit this (because Richard received thirty-two stitches from being stabbed in the back), but my dad getting assaulted ended up being a dream come true.

Yeah, in the beginning, a little trouble brewed in that Mother had lied to Richard about who fathered Marnie and me. Heck, she lied to Marnie and me about it as well. We thought we had the same father — some sailor who popped a wheelie then drove his motorcycle into a ravine. It never dawned on anyone that Marnie and I had different fathers or that one of them was related to someone "important." Besides, whoever Lou Greenshield was, he'd never contacted me or shown an ounce of interest. And he sure as heck never helped me with multiple-step equations, barbequed my favorite ribs, or made emergency trips to the store when I ran out of pads.

Mother gave us a sob story about how the Greenshield sons (Arthur and Eugene) had a falling out and how Eugene (my biological father) got flattened under a cement truck when he attempted to steal it. The family didn't want anything to do with her, so after the funeral, they packed her stuff and moved her to an apartment in faraway Bakersfield. We felt sorry for Mother, and the matter was dropped. Two days after her tearful confession, Richard and Mom held hands as our family strolled along the shoreline of Pismo Beach.

Okay, I confess there was a time or two (or ten) that I wondered about Eugene Greenshield. I was curious about what he looked like and who he was, besides the getting flattened part. I also wondered about the Greenshield clan. What kind of people would pack the property of a pregnant human being and dispose of her like a piece of trash? But I sure as heck never said anything or asked any questions. I loved Richard too much and didn't want to jeopardize our bond.

29

THE LIGHT GRAY SEDAN

January 1995

S even months later, life had a new normal. Marnie mastered a few tricks on the skateboard. Jimmy Jay could almost do the opening of "Stairway to Heaven" on his guitar. And I was in the best shape of my life, with a clear complexion and an increased ability to hold notes. Unfortunately, I still lacked enthusiasm, confidence, and skill. All of that changed on the day of the light gray sedan.

Rehearsal was mid-session when a car no one recognized parked along the curb. An unfamiliar couple opened the doors and proceeded to get out.

"You need assistance?" Jimmy Jay called to them.

The man shut his door and checked on us while the woman collected something from the back seat. Now, I gotta say this man was the tallest, darkest person I'd ever seen.

"This the McGee residence?"

"Y-y-y-y-yes," I responded.

"You McGee's kids?" The man's voice sounded funny — not stutter funny, funny like something was off.

"Why are you asking?" Jimmy Jay ventured.

The man's wife joined him, holding a tightly bundled newborn.

"Ooooooh," Marnie squealed, "you have a baby! Is it a boy or a girl?"

The woman smiled. "*She's* a girl." And then the mother tilted the blanketed bundle, giving Marnie a glimpse of curly-topped cuteness.

As Marnie admired the baby, I noticed the man seemed like something was off. His fingers trembled. He breathed funny. He kept blinking, and I swear it seemed as though he was about to have some sort of breakdown.

The door to the house opened, and Richard stepped out. "Hey," Richard greeted, "how are ya doing? Hope you're enjoying your time off as much as I did."

"IS THAT HIM?" the large man goaded. "IS THAT MCGEE?"

What does he mean? Is he mad at Richard?

His wife responded in a whisper.

Nobody talked. Nobody knew what was going on, so no one said anything. Then, this towering, huge goliath of a man stormed over to Richard, wrapped his arms around him, and picked him up in a massive bear hug. "Thank you! Thank you! With all of my heart and Jesus as my Savior, I must say thank you!"

"Put him down, Abraham," the woman exclaimed. "I swear, you're embarrassing me. You promised you wouldn't embarrass me. You're squeezing the poor guy. This guy saved my life. I brought you here to thank him, not squeeze the daylights out of him."

That's the officer my dad saved! Meyers is a woman!

The man put Richard down almost as if Richard were a porcelain doll. And then this big, fierce beast of a man openly wept in front of us.

"You don't know what this means to me. I'm so grateful for you and what you did. Thank you. Thank you for risking your life to save the love of mine. I know you saved that other officer also; that's good and all. I'm just grateful you saved my Laverne. What you done did that day is- is- is--"

"Of course," Richard returned, "no need to—"

"McGee," the woman cut in. She looked our way and explained. "Sorry, kids, we refer to ourselves by our last names at work. I'm Laverne Meyers. And this big old stubborn weeping willow is my husband, Abraham."

All of us kids said, "Hi."

"Anyhow, we're on this side of town, so we decided to stop by and introduce someone."

"I see," Richard uttered. "That's nice of—"

"Don't you get it!?!" Mr. Meyers burst into tears again.

What's he talking about? What's going on?

"What?" Jimmy Jay asked, intrigued. "What are we supposed to get?"

"Your dad didn't just save *two* lives in the office that day." Tears streamed down Mr. Meyers' hardy cheeks. "He saved *three*!"

Everyone turned to the baby.

"I suspected I was pregnant and confirmed it that day in the hospital," Laverne Meyers declared. "You didn't just save my life; you saved little Shanice here too."

By then, everyone felt a little overwhelmed, including me.

"What?" Richard gasped.

"You saved my wife and my daughter," Mr. Meyers groaned. "I'm indebted to you for life."

"Nah-nah-nah-nah-nah, none of that indebted stuff." Richard wiped a tear with the back of his hand. "Just enjoy every minute of being a dad. It's my reason for living." Richard looked down and shuffled his feet. "Ya wanna come in and stay for dinner? I'm about to fire up the grill and—"

"No, no, no, no! Thank you," Mrs. Meyers replied, "but we should be going. Just wanted to stop by and say Shanice is livin', breathing, and beautiful cause of you."

"Since my dad saved her life," Marnie quipped, "does that mean we're related? Is Shanice my new baby sister?"

Everyone chuckled.

"Truly," Mr. Meyers cut in, "if there's any way we can reciprocate or help in--"

"Nooo." Richard deflected, waving his hands. "Seeing Shanice is all the reward I need." He smiled sincerely. "Thank you. Thank you for this."

Richard and Mr. Meyers shook hands. Once again, Richard showed his humble side as the Meyers set out to leave. "Thank you for stopping by and making my day."

The Meyers family had almost reached their car when Mrs. Meyers paused, turned, and regarded Richard, wearing an intense, puzzled expression.

"What about your girl?" Mrs. Meyers pointed to me.

Me? What? What's she talking about?

As everyone stared at me, I shrank to the size of a chicken nugget.

"Her singing's good. She's talented in an unrefined, old-school kind of way, but she's lacking. Your lil' Miss here needs help. She needs mentoring. I think I've got the perfect idea. Something that'll help us feel we've done a good deed in return and benefit your little girl in the process."

"Ah, yeah, I guess," Richard returned. "What do you have in mind?"

"My Mamma's run choir at St. Thomas Baptist for thirty-seven years. They're world-famous and have won tons of awards. Do you think your little girl here would like to come and check it out?"

Richard turned to me for confirmation.

"Oh, heck, yeah," Marnie answered in my place, "I'll come too. Will our new baby sister be there?"

"It's a little early for Shanice. I'll probably keep her home for a while."

"Oh," Marnie's face scrunched, "it's a no-go for me. But Mitzy will be there. She needs bunches of help."

Everyone chuckled.

"What do you think?" Richard asked.

"I g-g-g-g-g-g-guess."

"Good," Mrs. Meyers beamed. "See you Sunday at ten."

30

ST. THOMAS BAPTIST

Mid-January 1995

S t. Thomas Baptist is a perfectly maintained architectural landmark
on Brundage Lane. Before I ventured there, I knew nothing about
the place. I didn't know Pastor Kenneth Ray Mulberry founded it sixty
years before or that it served generations of families with hope, faith,
nourished souls, and heaping servings of really good food.

Mother pulled to the curb out front seventeen minutes late.
"Okay, darling," she jested as she shifted into park. "Go on now, get to
experiencing."

"W-W-What? I thought y-y-you—"

"No, no, no, no, no, no. Nothing to do with them people being
Black. I ain't a racist. I gotta lotta flaws, but don't got a bigoted bone
in me. It's just me an' the Lord got some hashing out to do."

My hand gripped the door handle.

"Go on now, get. I ain't gonna sit here and—"

"B-B-B-But I-I-I-I'm—"

"I don't have time, Mitzy. You can do this."

I took a big breath, opened the door, and slid out of my seat.
Within a half-second of shutting the door, Mother shifted into gear

and took off. Her fancy Christmas Escalade gleamed gold as it sped out of the lot.

Please, nobody notices me! I pleaded as I started up the steps. *I hope nobody sees me. I just want to go in, get a seat, and stay stealth.*

When I got to the door, I turned the knob quietly so it didn't make the slightest noise. I didn't even breathe as I entered the massive expanse of a structure. No one saw me. No one stirred. Pastor Cole was mid-lecture in a lively sermon about faith next to thirty to forty choir members on a wood-planked stage.

I took a couple of steps (and was about to slide onto the finely polished surface of the back pew) when I tripped over a basket. Coins clattered along the aisle as I plunged into the woman in front of me, almost knocking her down.

"Oh! Oh! Oooooooh!" she wailed.

I awkwardly steadied myself while the poor woman retrieved her songbook. And then I heard a strange, synchronous shuffling as the congregation (all three hundred and forty) turned in their pews. The preaching stopped. The amens stopped. A kid stopped fussing. And I think I peed a little when I realized everyone was staring at me. All of them. All the parishioners in the entire church. All three hundred and forty men, women, and children.

"Are you okay, Miss Ruby?" Pastor Cole called from his pulpit.

"Yeah, just-just straightening up." She adjusted her hairpiece. "Gimme a minute."

"What about you?"

Everyone knew he meant me. As the congregation awaited my response, time spurred in a million directions. I couldn't talk. My stupid speech disorder had me tongue-tied and terrified.

When it became awkward, Miss Ruby spouted, "Y-Y-Yes, Pastor Cole. P-p-p-poor thing's a bit rattled. Brother Oliver left the o-offering basket in the aisle again."

She stutters! She stutters like me! She's not afraid of it.

"What's your name, young lady?" Pastor Cole called to me. "Have you ever been to..."

"Pastor Cole." Abraham. Meyers proudly rose to a stand. "She's the one!"

The entire congregation gasped. A frenzy of murmurs grew as parishioners bobbed in their pews to get a better look at me.

No, no, no, no, this isn't happening.

"Ladies and gentlemen," Mr. Meyers announced, "this is Mitzy McGee."

I think I just peed a little more.

"Her father saved Laverne and baby Shanice. Miss McGee's here for some faith and fellowship, and Laverne wants her to join the choir."

The brightly robed choir people stiffened to statues. A few brows smoldered while a girl in the front row protested with a scrunched nose.

"W-W-W-Well," Miss Ruby snapped. "Welcome her already!"

A smattering of applause started but quickly fizzled to silence.

No, no, no, no! This is definitely not invisible.

"Well then, McGee," Pastor Cole quipped, "come on down and make yourself at home."

Little did I know the magnitude of the moment as I trudged to the stage. I was too busy worrying about stumbling again or leaving a trail of urine on the floor.

* * *

A minute or so later, I stood amongst the choir as we sang a vibrant gospel classic. I'd heard it sometime in my past but couldn't remember the words for the life of me. Not knowing what else I should do, I tried to keep up but ended up singing the wrong words and returning to the wrong verses. *This is bad. This is really bad. This is a disaster. Never again will I walk on a stage without knowing all the words to a song. They're in matching robes, while I'm in a plaid shirt and khakis. This is not where I belong.*

But as the song progressed, their deep, rich harmonizations wrapped me in surreal holiness. Their tenors, pitches, and passion moved me to a place I never knew existed. Then – when I thought it couldn't get any better – the choir softly hummed as the matronly con- ductor (the lady with white hair and a gold-trimmed robe) went solo.

That's the monumental moment I first heard Miss Mayme Tucker sing. Mayme Tucker (Laverne Meyers' mother) had a voracious way of attacking a song. It wasn't perfect. No, perfect was stifled and stiff. Perfect lacked feeling. Perfect attacked the anatomy of structure, setting imagination aside. Miss Mayme's voice filled every nook and cranny of the room with gut-wrenched passion and grit.

As Miss Mayme sang, my heart rose into the light cast from the stained-glass windows, where I floated in the ambiance of colors, feeling the vibrancy of each pitch.

Thank you, God. Thank you. This is the music of my soul.

31

BEAUTY SCHOOL

February 1995

Halfway through my 8th-grade year, my mother did something amazing. She enrolled in school — beauty school, to be precise. I couldn't believe it. Ever since she married Richard, she'd carried on as if she didn't have a financial worry in the world. I don't know if the decision spawned from her and Richard's tension. Perhaps she was bored with little to do but clean house and shop for the past four and a half years. And it may have had something to do with contacting Lou Greenshield; maybe connecting with her youth revived her childhood dreams. But I honestly couldn't think of a better profession for someone obsessed with appearance.

So, I was happy. Super happy. I spearheaded our families' support, welcoming the change. To me, it would be great for the rest of us. It would get her out of the house, out of our hair (so to speak), and into doing something she loved. Unfortunately, my lamebrain didn't realize the danger of living with a beauty school protégée.

*   *   *

It happened on a regular, run-of-the-mill Saturday. All I did was walk in the kitchen.

"Mitzy, darling," she stood at the table, "you're just in time!"

On the center of the tablecloth sat a see-through tote of beauty school supplies.

"Come, come, come, let me show you what I got!"

"Oh-oh y-y-y-yeah."

"This morning, they issued our supplies. There's so much good stuff here. Have a seat; I can't wait to show you!"

Gosh, she's so happy.

"Look, they have clips and combs and shears, and look at this here fancy beautician's poncho."

"W-w-w-wow, that's a-a-a lot."

"It is, isn't it?" She draped the cape around my shoulders and began to fasten the snaps. "Let's see how it fits."

I'm glad she's happy and has all this great stuff.

"This is fun," she beamed. "I'm lucky to have two lovely daughters who support my dream."

She gathered my long, wavy hair from beneath the cape and combed it along my back. My mother had mad skills with a hairbrush; each stroke was a litany of care.

"Now, I'm just gonna spray a little conditioner so it's easier to trim."

"Trim!?! N-N-N-N-No. I-I-I-I-I—"

"Stop being silly," she chuckled. "I'm just gonna cut half an inch. Okay, maybe an inch. But your hair's so long, no one will notice. I need practice; I really do. Besides, what I see here is split-end city. It's damaged and—"

"O-O-Only an inch?"

"Yes, of course."

Forty-five seconds later, I heard the first *tchac-tchac* of scissors trimming my hair. And then I heard *tchac-tchac, tchac-tchac, tchac-tchac.*

It's only an inch. It's only an inch. She's in beauty school; it's good to support her. This feels nice. Wait that felt higher than an inch. It feels—

Marnie strolled through my line of vision as she ventured to the refrigerator. Except Marnie wasn't Marnie because Marnie had shoulder-length sandy-brown hair. Marnie was cute. Marnie was adorable. Marnie was a fairy princess. The elf-like imposter who selected a juice bottle had a short, hacked-off do that sprang from her head in bushels and spouts.

"M-M-Marnie, what h-h-h-happened to-to-to your h-h-hair?"

Tchac-tchac, tchac-tchac tchac-tchac.

"Oh, that." Marnie stopped in front of me. Instead of pouring a glass, she drank directly from the juice bottle. "Mom gave me a trim. Looks good, huh?"

"W-w-w-w-what?"

No, Marnie, you look like you've been electrocuted. It looks horrible. It looks really, really—

"I look like Blanche from 'The Golden Girls.'"

Tchac-tchac, tchac-tchac tchac-tchac.

I shuddered.

"Shoot. Mitzy, be still! What'd I tell you? You made me mess up again."

Tchac-tchac, tchac-tchac tchac-tchac.

"Now, I have to start over!"

Twenty–two minutes later – twenty-two minutes of *tchac-tchac, tchac-tchacs* and startovers – and a considerable portion of my long, luxurious mane lay scattered along the cold kitchen linoleum. I wanted to get up. I wanted to run for my life, but I had no self-esteem. Besides, I didn't want to disappoint my mother. When I finally got a chance to check my hair in the mirror, my heart filled with grief. *Well, I figured, at least she's consistent. She gave Marnie a "Blanche" and me a "Rose."*

That evening at dinner – as we sat around the table, waiting for Jimmy Jay – I waded in remorse. Mother had traumatized the entire family. Poor Marnie's hair looked like a goat got goat rabies. I looked like a frisky seventy-year-old while Richard's sideburns were cockeyed and three inches off. And he had this fluffy peacock poof on the top of his head.

It was so weird: I thought I'd entered a beautician's version of the zombie apocalypse. And then the most shocking thing happened: the stunner of stunners. The door from the garage opened, and Jimmy Jay strolled in, sporting his newly trimmed and tailored hairstyle. Except Jimmy Jay's hair didn't look like an electrified poodle. It didn't look like a drowned elf. And it didn't look like a… (I'm sorry, but I don't know how to describe Richard's monstrosity — a peacock in heat?) No. Honestly – as I live and breathe – Jimmy Jay's hair had been cropped to a shag that framed his face to a tee. All the permed and damaged ends were gone. All the gold — gone. Jimmy Jay's hair looked healthy and radiant and good. Fantastic even. It was the best I'd seen his hair. Jimmy Jay looked like a rock star of rock stars.

"Mom," Jimmy Jay asked once he slid into his seat, "can you pass the pepper."

"Sure," she replied.

As she handed him the plastic pepper mill, I fumed. *It's not fair. It's really not fair. She practiced on us, and I guess she got better.*

"JJ, what'd the guys think of your trim?" Mother asked.

"They like it. They said you did a good job."

"Of course, they like it," she squealed. "You look phenomenal!"

"They all volunteered to go next."

"*Ahem! Ahem!*" Richard fake coughed.

"Except no one wants a Golden Girl or Correctional Officer; they all want shags like mine."

Mother smiled and ate. Jimmy Jay smiled and ate. Marnie didn't notice anyone's mood; she was too busy sneaking Brussels sprouts into a napkin (to be flushed). And while everyone sat happy dorky, Richard and I sank into our seats, staring at each other. Part of me wanted to cry, but then Richard winked at me. I laughed, and he laughed, and it turned into one of those Father-Daughter folds in time that took the sting out of cruddy hair. That's my dad. Richard just had a way of making things better.

32

SINGING OUTSIDE THE LINES

April 1995

T he next month or so drifted in a slow, steady stream of teenage angst. Mother practiced her haircutting skills. Within weeks, Marnie and I had matching Pomeranians while Jimmy Jay and the guys sported radically different dos. And I had to admit that with each trim and style, Mother improved -- oh, except for Richard. Richard didn't look good in Mother's haircuts. He *never* looked good in Mother's haircuts. Some were outright ghastly. Week after week, he came to the table donning the angry monkey, the panther testicle, and the constipated cockatoo.

We let Mother practice on us even though she could be horrible because that's what families do. They stand by each other with support even when they go to work and become the laughingstock of the prison. That's what Richard taught us. He taught us family is more important than anything.

* * *

And as we went around in hairstyles that didn't suit our person-alities, Jimmy Jay and the crew sported spikes, pompadours, and shags in varying lengths and fluffiness. The guys suddenly went from cute musical geeks to neighborhood dreamboats. That's when the pretty parade turned into a mixed-match assortment of outright groupies.

2-Tall was the first to get a girlfriend. He had long since crushed on a volleyball player from school. Once Desiree Kemp saw Purple Bucket Gumption, her attraction to the tall, spindly guitarist flew over the moon. They talked after practice and were smitten by the end of the day.

Jimmy Jay and Chris were next, except they didn't stick with one person — such is the life of an aspiring rock star. Jimmy Jay and Chris chatted with them all. They had no preference for age, height, or hair color as they flirted with various fans in the groupie pool. Jimmy Jay and Chris soon earned monikers as neighborhood tramp-a-lots.

*   *   *

At the time, there was this massive attraction between Billy and me; at least, that's the way I saw it. We talked every once in a while and somehow became friends. Since I've known him, Billy has never – not once – harmed my self-esteem. Besides his heaven-sent dimples, maybe that's why I crushed on him. I don't know. All I know is Billy's the only band brother who made it to St. Thomas when I had my first solo.

"Wow, Mitz, something's happened. Your voice has qualities I never heard before." Billy stood in the red-carpeted corridor by the choir room. "I used to dig your perfect tone and rhythm, but there's something more. Seriously, I've never heard runs like that. The way you twirl notes is unbelievable. Where'd all this come from?"

A lot of people, I yearned to say.

It's practicing five times a week with Miss Mayme Tucker. Miss Mayme's shown me decades of expertise in Gospel, Soul, and R&B. She's taught me to go against the rules, read between notes, and lead with my heart. She's given me the gift of singing outside the lines.

It's the guidance and support of a choir of uniquely brilliant people. At first, I didn't fit in, but my choir family soon accepted me as one of their own.

Miss Ruby has shown me it's possible not to let my stutter define me.

It's working out every day to improve my endurance.

It's eating the right foods and keeping myself hydrated.

It's the zillion hours I've spent listening to songstresses, from the classics to chart-topping singles.

All of this, I did thinking of you.

Unfortunately, I didn't say any of that. The thirteen-year-old version of me was tongue-tied and shy.

"I-I-I d-d-don't know," I gushed, embarrassed. "Gee-Gee-Gee, thanks."

Billy smiled and nodded politely. That's as far as our companionship thing went. I wouldn't put Billy in the friend zone; we were bandmates and closer than that. But I confess here and now my crush on that boy was a massive motivator that inspired me to succeed.

Funny how love can lift you one day. It can have you singing in front of three hundred and forty people, even when your hair's cut like a fashion poodle. It can have you talking in school, even volunteering to answer a teacher's questions. It can have you tell Desiree DeCampo to "S-S-S-S-Stop with the crude-crude c-c-c-comments and-and-and-and grow a life." And it can have you not objecting when Tarantula Tramp Stamps signed up to perform at the Kern County Fair, where I would sing in front of Bakersfieldians from all over Kern County.

Unfortunately, six weeks before the fair performance, love took my heart from the highest peak of the highest mountain and smashed it to the ground. And that's when love did the cruelest thing imaginable. Love stepped on my heart, wearing stupid pink sandals with stupid pink bows.

33

PINK-SANDALED GHOUL

August 1995

B eing in a band meant we hung out. After Billy went to my solo at St. Thomas, the guys attended several church events where I sang. At the time, I belonged to the choir at St. Thomas, the choir at school, and a specialty ensemble with the Bakersfield Music Theatre. But it wasn't just about me. Rebellious Puppets also attended Chris's grandpa's funeral, 2-Tall's sister's baptism, Jimmy Jay's video game championship, and Billy Bearheart's pow-wow.

The pow-wow, I remember it as if it were yesterday. It took place the summer after my 8th-grade year. I remember the music. I remember the food. Most of all, I remember walking up to the concession stand and seeing bad Billy Bearheart at the register with NO SHIRT ON. *Ay Yi Yi*, I mean, really!

Don't know if I had a bad bladder or what, but the second he looked at me with those perfectly taut abs, I about let out the Niagara Falls of all gushers. As I said, bad Billy Bearheart is one good-looking Native American.

"Hey, Mitz," he greeted, "glad you made it."

"Of c-c-c-course," I replied, trying my best not to stare at his torso.

"Whatcha gonna order?"

"Oh-Oh-Oh, y-yeah, umm…"

Don't stare! Don't look at his abs. They're something, but don't look. Don't stare at his pecs, either. They're perfect, like literally perfect. Oh, look, I've never seen Billy's nipples before. I know he has nipples; of course, he has nipples. But this is a first. They're masculine and... Wait, hurry and order.

"I-I'd like a soda and s-s-s-s-some nipples."

"Did she say NIPPLES?" squealed the red-haired cashier beside him.

"N-N-N-N-N-No, I-I-I-I—"

"I heard you!" she announced loud enough for everyone to hear. "You said NIPPLES!"

Nearby patrons turned and gawked at me. A grandmotherly type gave me a scorned sneer while a disgruntled couple ushered their children to the other side of the concession stand.

"I meant to-to-to say nachos."

"Nachos," Billy repeated, "good. Did you want the mild sauce or one with pretty hot jalapenos?"

"I-I-I like it hot-hot-hot-hot."

"WHAT?" Red-haired shrieked. "She says she likes it hot! Hot! Hot! Hot! Man, Bearheart, she's really into you. Is she a pow-wow groupie or a groupie from your band?"

"She's not a groupie," Billy frowned, "she's my friend."

"Okay," she muttered as she passed a basket of fries to her customer. "If you say so."

"Which soda would you like with that?"

"Can I have a Dr. P-P-P-Pecker?"

"What?" Red-haired shrieked again.

Oh, no, what have I done? I meant to say Pepper. Dr. Pepper. This darn stutter and Billy's chest have me tongue-tied and embarrassed.

"I-I-I-I—"

"Listen, whatever your name is—"

"Her name's Mitzy," Billy cut in. "She's my friend. She has a stutter, and she's the lead singer of my band, so don't say anything mean."

And that's when this red-haired girl, this hobgoblin-beast of a person, this monster vampire wolf-faced *troll*, said the worst thing imaginable. Her words cut into my chest, ripped out my heart, then splayed it across the ground for everyone to bear witness.

"Aww, sweetie." Red hair came out from behind the concession stand and approached me, taking tiny, delicate steps in her tiny, delicate sandals. "I'm *sorry!*" she cooed as she wrapped her arms around me. "I feel so bad, you poor thing. Billy's a bad boyfriend for not introducing us and telling me you had a stutter."

Wait! What?

"Billy, sweetheart. Give her whatever she wants -- my treat."

"I-I-I-I—"

"Oh, there's no need to thank me, Marsha. I'm—"

"M-M-M-M-Mitzy."

"Oh, dear, it must be tough. You poor thing."

Billy handed me my order, and for a split-second, I considered dropping it on Red-hair's shoes. Then I realized it was something my mother would have done, so I collected my nachos and soda without letting go of anything.

"Jaslene's gonna come to practice," Billy announced. "She's volunteered to film Tarantula Tramp Stamps at the fair."

Hold the nachos. It's okay if I drop the soda; just don't drop the nachos.

"Actually, I'm glad the two of you finally get to meet." Billy smiled sincerely. "Got my two best girls here."

Drop the soda! Drop the soda!

"Y-y-y-yea," I muttered.

I should have left, but I couldn't. I felt a weird innate loyalty to Billy, so I stayed. I stayed and watched them take their shoes off and dance in the center of the drum circle. I stayed and watched as Billy introduced Jaslene to his family. And I stayed and saw them share a romantic handhold at sunset. The entire time, I felt torn. Part of me was glad for Billy because I'd never seen him so happy. However, a bigger part of me felt sick to my stomach with jealousy and regret. Jealousy and regret left a bad taste in my mouth and a lump in my belly.

*   *   *

The day after the pow-wow, Billy showed up at practice with his shiny new girlfriend.

Oh, good, I grumbled. *Now she shows up here. I hope she doesn't kiss him or get in my way.*

Jaslene settled into a folding chair. She leaned back with her small, black case perched on her lap when Marnie strolled into the garage, donning one of Mother's spikiest, most outlandish hairstyles.

"Oh, hey," Jaslene greeted my little sister. "You two," she pointed to Marnie and me, "must get your hair done at the same place."

"Yep," Marnie gushed as she plopped into the seat next to Jaslene.

Marnie focused on Jaslene's mysterious case as the guys positioned themselves for practice.

"What's that?" Marney's face scrunched.

"It's a camcorder," Jaslene said proudly. "I promised Billy-Bearbaby I'd record your fair performance. But I thought I'd try it out now so you can see how you look."

"That'd be awesome!" 2-Tall announced.

"Yeah," Chris Lee seconded. "It'd be cool to see what we look like while we play."

"Definitely," Billy chimed, "my girl's got some great ideas."

"Y-Y-Y-Y-Y-Yeah," I grunted, "but, but..."

Before I could voice my objection, Billy drummed the intro to one of our ballads. And the next thing I knew, we were mid-song. My brain spun as I stood behind the microphone - glaring at Jaslene and belting out lyrics. *Listen to this!*

When the song finished, Marnie applauded. The groupies applauded. Even the guys applauded as they swaggered around the garage, sharing high-fives and praise. Everyone seemed happy —

everyone, that is, except Jaslene. Jaslene's expression melted as if the grim reaper stood in the middle of the garage, practicing putts with his trusty scythe.

"What's wrong?" Billy asked when he finally noticed.

"Well..." Jaslene looked hesitant. "Ah, sort of... Well, a couple of things."

She's full of it. I sang great. The guys were great. It's a fantastic song.

"It's not your music." Jaslene looked down while she collected her words. "You guys are good, really good. Maybe even become famous and strike it rich kinda good."

"Then what's the problem?" 2-Tall questioned with furrowed brows.

"Well, honestly – and I mean this in the nicest way – I'm going to start with Mitzy. Mitzy's voice has this Janis Joplin, Etta James type of thing, and she's standing there with a Peter Pan hairstyle. Not trying to be mean here, but it's a distraction."

Peter Pan!?! WHAT!?!

"And..." 2-Tall coaxed in an edged tone.

"And none of you move."

"What?"

"It's not a performance if none of you move. Billy twirls drumsticks and grooves in his chair, but the rest of you stand as if you're glued to the floor."

"What else," Jimmy Jay asked between gritted teeth.

"Mitzy," she directed her attention to me, "as lead singer, you – especially you – must get into the music. You need to entertain. You know, dance. Move to the groove. Flip your hair. Pop a pose. Most importantly, you gotta make eye contact with the audience. You can't stand still and not connect on a song like that."

"You should go," Jimmy Jay snapped.

"Yeah," 2-Tall seconded, "I'm with him on that. No one talks to Mitzy that way."

"Babe," Billy shook his head remorsefully, "what'd I tell you? No one disrespects her; it's a rule. No one disrespects our girl."

"Sorry," Jaslene pleaded. "I'm so sorry. I just thought you wanted—"

"W-W-W-W-Wait!" I snapped. "I-I-I wanna see the video."

As the six of us huddled around Jaslene's tiny monitor, no one moved or said anything.

"Turn it o-o-o-off," I spouted halfway through the song.

Jaslene stood breathless.

"Sh-She's right," I declared. "Everything she said was s-s-s-spot on."

Jaslene's eyes welled as she fought back tears.

My face turned to meet the guys.

"We have six weeks until the f-f-f-fair. W-W-W-We've got-got to come t-together and fix this. And I'm pretty sure we're gonna n-n-n-need Jaslene's help."

34

KERN COUNTY FAIR

September 26, 1995

September 26, 1995, Tarantula Tramp Stamps performed to a packed house at the Kern County Fair. And, man-oh-man, it was great.

At first, our audience consisted of thirty to forty friends and family members. But once we got into a groove, dozens of fairgoers surrounded the stage. None of what happened next would have happened if it wasn't for some pretty awesome people.

Jimmy-Jay and 2-Tall got a lot of help from their guitar teacher, who ensured they played well and looked the part.

Billy Bearheart received his dad's new drum set, embossed with his tribe's insignia.

Chris Lee wore his first Mohawk, compliments of my mother. Chris's Mohawk perfected his transition from glee club choir boy to MTV rocker.

And I had a long list of people to thank. Miss Mayme Tucker reviewed my melodies and helped me whip them into something spectacular. She even offered her advice on how to "lay a little stank here and there." Miss Ruby lent me a colorful wig. Marnie selected my clothes: a pink sequined top (borrowed from Mother's closet), blue jean cutoffs, and boots. And I had Jaslene's assistance with presentation.

By the day of the fair, Jaslene and I formed a repertoire of stances and moves that I could do in front of an audience. I knew how to flip my hair, roll my shoulders, skip across the stage, and stop and pose in different ways to accentuate the song. Basically, Jaslene introduced me to the Art of Performance. We spent so much time getting ready for the fair that by the time the day arrived, Jaslene and I were – more or less – friends. It sounds weird, I know, especially because I still crushed on Billy Bearheart. Nevertheless, Jaslene Bautista was my first female friend and Billy's steady. I guess when it comes to being in a band, relationships can be kind of messy.

And there's another person I gotta thank: Richard. Right before we got on stage (minutes before we performed), Richard came backstage and caught me amid a grappling attack of stage fright. I stood there, sweating, shaking, and feeling like I would pee and barf at the same time. That's when my dad said the magic words that secured my seat on the ride to stardom.

"You can be the rockstar you want; you just gotta fake it till you make it."

"W-W-W-What?"

"Listen, when I first started as an officer, they stuck me in the worst unit in the prison. It was me and two hundred of the meanest convicted felons in the state. Those guys were horrible. They were two and three times my size, and they were experts at fighting and killin people. And the thing they hated most in the world is fresh correctional officer meat."

"What did-did-did you do?"

"Shoot, I was only twenty-four and a rookie, but I didn't want to quit. Sarah was pregnant with Leiann, and I couldn't let them down. So, I decided to do something crazy. I marched into the unit and took control by pretending to be the greatest correctional officer in the world. I acted as though I wasn't intimidated. I acted as though nothing and no one bothered me. I just did my job like the actor in me thought was right, incorporating professionalism, wit, and spunk. Within time, I became Slick Rick. Officers and inmates respected me because I became the part everyone wanted."

"Are you saying I should pretend I'm a rock star?"

He shook his head and winked at me.

"And give them what they want."

"Mitz," Jimmy Jay shouted, "it's time!"

Basically, that's how I ended up on stage at the Kern County Fair, singing my heart out as if I were the greatest singer of all time. I sang like a pro. I performed. I gave them professionalism, spunk, and a little razzle-dazzle. I emulated the rock star everyone wanted to see. The entire experience felt amazing. The guys did a fantastic job, I did a fantastic job, and we had fun. By the time we wrapped up, three or four hundred spectators surrounded the stage, hooting and hollering with rip-roaring flair. And I gotta admit, once I released my first note, my stage fright checked out for the night, and the only person left was this icon of a person I always had inside me but never knew.

*   *   *

Eight minutes after our performance, our world turned upside down. As we stood backstage, congratulating each other on a job well done, a small-statured man in gray pants and a pink stretchy top asked if he could speak with our manager.

"That's me," Chris announced. "How can I help?"

"Actually," the man retorted, "I may be able to help you. I'm Mac Michaels. I have a label in LA. I'd like you to come down and show me some of your tracks. Maybe we can work out a deal."

SECTION IV

AGES FOURTEEN TO SEVENTEEN

35

TERRANCE DANIEL FORESTER, III

August 1996

Etta Sabrina-Louise Forester had long since mapped the road for her son's success. Beginning with an anticipated congressional appointment in his senior year of school, Terrance Daniel Forester, III (a handsome, soft-spoken, respectful young man), would attend officer candidate school with the United States Navy. After a successful stint as an officer, Terrance would go on to graduate school, where he'd earn his doctorate in philosophy or any other subject that earned a voice in this world. Then, he'd construct a platform and become the world's greatest human rights advocate. The plan had been forged since he was a newborn with a cute curly fro and tuxedo diaper.

Only one thing stood in her way. Something the headstrong professor from CSUB never anticipated. Her beloved son befriended a ragtag group of rabble-rousers who somehow learned to play music and formed a band.

Now, Etta Forester prided herself as a sensible woman. However, she saw no sense in the nonsense of dropping his hopes and dreams to chase something impossible like catching a star. She loved her Terrance almost as much as she hated the moniker 2-Tall. That's why she agreed to let him continue his hobby as a musician, but only until he left for the military.

That meant we had one year to develop our album, sign with Mac Michaels, record our tracks, and become rich — or everything we worked so hard for would have gone to waste. 2-Tall was the heart and soul of our band; we wouldn't be the same without him. So, at the beginning of that school year (2-Talls last at Stockdale), we spent a bazillion hours in the garage. We mulled over notes, harmonies, and lyrics as we bashed brains trying to develop tracks for our album. We soon learned top ten singles didn't materialize from thin air.

"You guys are fantastic," Mac Michaels had said two days after the fair. "I'll sign you when you produce something I can use." He sat at a desk before a large bay window, overlooking an enormous pool surrounded by white pedestaled cabanas in his Beverly Hills mansion/studio. "Go back to Bakersfield and create something fantastic. Make it stuff kids your age can relate. It's always good to include the standards of happiness, heartbreak, hardship, and that sort of thing, but go with your gut."

"Will we have a say in video production?" Chris Lee asked.

"Of course, but we're getting ahead of ourselves. For now, you need to come up with eight to ten songs. If they're good, I'll sign your band, and we'll start recording."

We beamed with excitement.

"No, no, no, no, no," Mac downplayed, "don't get your hopes in a tizzy. This will take a lot of work. It won't come easy. Here, let me tell you: if you stick together, value everyone's contribution, and give a hundred percent, then you have a slight chance – let's say one in a thousand – of recording something that makes the charts. This isn't easy. It's breaking brains. It's learning to compromise. And it's collaborating with people who'll get on your nerves."

We stood stone-faced. None of us expected to hear this.

"But," Mac continued, "nothing's like standing on stage in front of thirty-thousand screaming spectators. Nothing's like having a voice regarding world peace, dirty politics, or whatever suits your fancy. And nothing's like having a pile of money in your bank account. What can I say? Nothing compares to making it big."

Later that night (after we returned from Mac Michaels' estate), Jimmy Jay took a can of spray paint and inscribed *Nothing Compares to Making it Big* on our garage wall. It became our band motto.

36

LEMONS TO CHAMPAGNE

October 31, 1996

H alloween that year was something spectacular. Since it was the guy's last year at Stockdale, Mom and Dad let Jimmy Jay have a gathering at the house to celebrate his birthday. Unfortunately (for Mom, Dad, and nearby neighbors), that small gathering grew to nearly a hundred teens. Eventually – well before the ten o'clock homeowners' association curfew – we brought out our instruments and played our first song.

As everyone stood and sat around, Marnie (in a ninja costume) entertained the crowd with various kicks, chops, and princess stances. None of what she did resembled martial arts, yet she looked incredible as she had the time of her life. Marnie didn't care what anyone thought. It was her brother's birthday, so she chopped, kicked, and twirled with everything she had.

And it was then – as the crowd lost interest in our tormented tale of love and betrayal – that Jimmy Jay morphed the melody. Inspired by Marnie's antics, Jimmy Jay started singing from the top of his head.

"Kung-Fu girl can kick your butt. She can knock you out and songster strut. Fly a rocket to the moon. No limit to what this girl can do."

We joined in and made it the new chorus. Pretty soon, everyone rocked out to "Kung-Fu Girl." Partygoers repeatedly requested it, so we played it again and again. When the party ended, everyone went home, happy and amazed — or so we thought.

*   *   *

The next morning, I awoke to an ear-piercing noise from downstairs. "OH, NO! Noooo!" Mother screeched. "This can't be! This CAN'T BE!"

Marnie and I rushed to the kitchen and found Mother in her mud mask and rollers with a crazed expression. "What have you done?"

"What do you mean," Marnie asked, and then she opened the cupboard and selected a cereal box.

"This!" Mother shook a newspaper. "This is a disaster. What will the neighbors think? What will my friends think? What if my customers at the beauty shop see this? Oh, Lord, Belinda, my boss... This will give her something to gloat about."

Mother turned to me. "What is this!?!"

My brain backfired when I saw the headline. *Local band performs a culturally insensitive concert, offending African and Asian Americans.* The article featured a photograph of Marnie doing a kick in front of Chris Lee, who came to the party dressed as a tin man. However, the way the picture was situated and cropped (and the fact that Chris had taken off his aluminum foil hat) made it appear that Chris's silver face paint was blackface. And it got worse. The article described the lyrics of Kung-Fu Girl as an anthem of hate.

The phone rang.

"Hello?" Mother answered. "Oh, hello, Etta. Yes, I saw it. No, we're not racists. No, that's not what we allow them to... No, it was a costume. It's not a Klan costume; it's a kimono. It's... It's..."

By seven, the phone had gone off a half dozen times. Etta Forester threatened to hire an attorney and take 2-Tall out of the band. Richard had been summoned to the prison to speak with officials from personnel investigations while a national news affiliate offered financial compensation to do a story on "the kids singing the hate song." Basically, all our work and dreams were on the verge of destruction.

"Well," Marnie quipped as she poured another bowl of cereal. By then, Jimmy Jay had joined us at the table. "… at least the band's out there. Isn't that what all of you wanted — to get a lucky break? Now you've got the publicity; all you gotta do is change it around. You gotta take the lemons, pour a buttload of sugar on them, and make sugar-sweetened lemonade!"

"You're right," Jimmy Jay agreed. "Somehow, we've gotta turn this into something we can use."

*   *   *

Four o'clock that afternoon, Mother was at work deflecting the story (probably blaming Leiann). Richard was at the prison. Etta Sabrina-Louise Forester was at her attorney's office. And Chris and Billy's parents sat at a table at Olive Garden, fuming with rage. And while all that happened, Rock Pudding called a press conference in the garage. We invited all of them: local news stations, national news stations (procuring financial compensation), and our local newspaper (with affiliates worldwide).

At our conference, Chris Lee displayed photos of himself in his Tin Man costume from Halloween night. He admonished a local journalist for editing the image until it appeared horrific and unspeakable. Marnie displayed her outfit and the bag it was purchased in, verifying it was merely a child's Halloween costume. Lastly, and most importantly, Rock Pudding (my idea for the name) put on an impromptu concert, which we rehearsed for most of the day.

Instead of "Kung-Fu Girl," we changed the title and catchphrase to "Millennial Girl." We slowed the chorus to make it chorale-like. And we modified the lyrics to make it an anthem for female empowerment. The new version wasn't just good; it was incredible!

By the end of the week, Rock Pudding made front-page news in every newspaper, news magazine, and news story worldwide. We had seventeen record companies vying for us to sign, yet we signed with Mac Michaels even though we only had one song under our belt.

* * *

Two months later, "Millennial Girl" circuited radio stations as a top ten hit. Kids sang it in school. We had award shows. We had talk show appearances. And we raked in our first batch of dough. However, Etta Sabrina-Louise Forester said it wasn't enough; 2-Tall remained on the roster to attend officer candidate school that fall. All the while, Mac Michaels only accepted two of our songs: "Millennial Girl" and "American Heroes Like Leiann." As far as we were concerned, we had to come up with eight stellar tracks. And we had to do it fast.

37

JUGGLING JIGGLES

Summer 1997

Jimmy Jay, Marnie, and I sat stuffed in the back of Mother's Escalade as she carted us to Beverly Hills for a meeting with Mac Michaels. It had been ten months since "Millennial Girl" first played on the radio, and - for some reason- Mother thought she was entitled to a chunk of the money.

"When I get my share," Mother announced, "I'm gonna open my own beauty shop. Everything's gonna be pink, and I'm gonna have a wine refrigerator, a gold-plated nose hair plucker, and massage chairs that flatten fat globs and cellulite. It'll be fancy with a bunch of cool stuff."

"You're entitled to *your* share, Mrs. McGee," Mac said as his secretary handed Mother a fresh cocoa latte. "I don't know what contracts you've signed; just have your attorney provide a notarized copy of your paperwork, and I'll--"

Mother shook her head.

"Oh, you don't have a..."

Mother looked concerned.

"Oh, okay, well, I see. Let me spell this out for you. First, you're not entitled to anything from JJ (Jimmy Jay). He turns eighteen soon; he'll be an adult."

Mother's brows sank. "But I—"

"I know. I know," Mac sympathized. "You're the one who's cooked and cared for the lad. I agree you should receive something for that. But the law says..."

Mother looked sick.

"And when it comes to Mitzy, here. She signed an agreement in compliance with federal mandates and child labor laws that places her portion of the band's earnings into a trust until she's eighteen."

"What!?!" Mother gasped.

Mac Michaels steepled his fingers. "It's the law."

"You're kidding!" Mother snapped.

"Nope," he shrugged, "feel free to look it up yourself."

"This... This is..." Mother fumed. "This is an outrage."

"Would it be outrageous if I offer you $15,000.00 here and now as an advance towards Mitzy's eighteen-year-old profit?"

"Ahhh—"

"Not going to make this offer twice. You can take the $15,000.00 or see me in court, which could take years."

"Take the money, Mamma!" Marnie squealed. "Take the money! It's enough for your shop and your butt juggling chairs!"

"Make it $50,000.00," Mother countered, "and we've got ourselves a deal."

*   *   *

Once Jimmy Jay received a good chunk of change from appearance fees, profits from Millennial Girl, and the preliminary sales from Millennial Girl merchandise, he bought the house three doors down. He moved out and moved in the very next day. Things had become a little strained between him and our mom, so moving like that was a good idea. In the meantime, we still huddled in the family garage (amongst Sarah McGee's boxed effects) until the built-ins, sound-proofing panels, and electrical circuits were outfitted at his new place.

Mother resented us using *her* property, but she was gone most of the time (setting up her new salon), so it didn't matter. Dad, on the other hand, couldn't have been more proud. Even though Marnie and I were no longer little, he still knocked on our bedroom door and bid us a good night before he left for his graveyard shift at the prison. Sometimes, he planted peck kisses on our foreheads. Others he cracked the door (wearing his correctional officer uniform) and caught me scribbling in my journal.

"Write something amazing," he'd say. "Write something that'll bring the world to its knees." "10-33 'em lyrics with a yard-stomping beat that'll knock 'em away!"

The next four and a half months were a brain-numbing, pains-taking, argument-riddled nest of appearances, gigs, and photoshoots — all while attempting to complete our album. And I must say here and now, there's something about crafting words into songs that I found amazing. Grasping the finesse of language, I realized how words encompassed a form of art, including rhyme, refrain, imagery, metaphors, and a bunch of junk I had yet to understand.

Spending a lot of time in the library, in the back pew of St. Thomas, and snuggled in bed next to Sarah McGee's mural, I melded words for five or six songs. I found the inspiration for another song in a journal entry from the sixth grade. The guys took my lyrics and melded them into music. Generally, the process took a couple of hours to a couple of weeks to perfect a song. One thing about Rock Pudding: our music was *always* a team effort, especially when it mattered the most.

* * *

On a mild-mannered September afternoon, eleven days before 2-Tall was slated to leave for officer candidate school, we discussed a news story about a white-on-black police shooting. The police officer stated he shot the suspect because he feared for his life; however, the news clip showed the suspect lying on his belly while the officer pulled out his gun and shot him in cold blood.

"Sometimes, I feel like a marked man." 2-Tall shook his head. "I can't go for a drive, walk, or jog in my neighborhood without taking the risk of being shot. It isn't right."

My brain spun as my fingers frantically searched for something to write with. "W-w-what do-do you mean?"

"I wish I could walk outside and be seen as myself, not a stereotype. Our generation is the one who can do it. Our generation can make this right."

*   *   *

Six days later – five days before 2-Tall left for officer candidate school – we had a jam session in the garage where we invited our families and friends. Of course, Richard was there. Mother, on the other hand, was a no-show in that she scrambled to complete the finishing touches on Victoria's Venus Boutique and Day Spa. Chris's parents were there, as well as his sisters. Billy had his mom and dad, who miraculously got along. Most importantly, Etta Sabrina-Louise Forester was in attendance with 2-Tall's grandmamma and four of his aunties.

During that concert, we played five songs we hoped to record, including: "Skateboarder's Anthem," "Making it Big," and "We Gotta Make This Right." During "We Gotta Make This Right" (a tribute to our generation regarding racial profiling and hate), Etta Forester beamed with pride.

"You did good," she gushed as she hugged her son. "Real good. I see how you can use this as a platform to promote change." Her eyes caramelized with joy. "I won't force officer candidate school. You can stay; I trust you kids will greatly impact the world."

That afternoon, we hung around with our families, discussing our hopes and dreams as Richard lit the grill. Pretty soon, Marnie started dancing. That's when Mother arrived and found Marnie on her back with her feet whirling in the air.

"Marnie," Mother gasped, "get up! Ladies don't do that; it's not—"

"Hey, Mama," Marnie stood and dusted her knees, "how'd it go with your big *penis?*"

Everyone froze as all eyes panned to our mother.

"Venus, Marnie!" Mother groaned. "Venus! I told you it's Victoria's *Venus* Boutique and Day Spa because I'm a Taurus. Taurus's are related to the bull and get things done."

Everyone nodded as if they finally got the meaning.

"Oh," Marnie replied. "I thought it was penis because bulls have big..."

38

MIRACLE OF THE MACHINE

October 1997

T enth grade was my favorite year in school. Some kids loved me; others shunned me, called me names, and belittled me whenever possible. That didn't matter because I had friends. I had real, true friends. Having friends made everything right.

The library was the same, though. The library was the same familiar oasis where I spent my time huddled at a desk, crafting language. That's the thing about writing. To me, words had colors and textures that worked like magic. The right words could give me tickles or tears, anguish or anger, or a sense of intrigue. The songsmith in me spent hours in that room, conquering the world.

Halfway through the school year, I'd crafted lyrics for fifteen potential songs. Mac Michaels had already approved our first four recordings; he patiently awaited the next six before we completed our album, filmed videos, and joined one of his bands on tour.

* * *

"Why are you late?" Mother snapped when I walked in the door at 6:30 p.m. "I just got in from the salon, and I'm bushed. I hoped you would have done something around here. You haven't done your chores. I mean, really, Mitzy. You could have come straight home from school and cooked dinner. Where were you? Were you wasting time in the library again?"

I looked down and shook my head affirmatively.

"What have I said about that? Now, I have to do everything, and—"

"I-I-I-I'm sorry," I cut in. "I'll load the washer and fry-fry up s-s-s-some ground b-b--."

"No worries," Marnie cut in as she trotted down the staircase, "I got it taken care of."

"What!?!" I gasped. The last time Marnie loaded the washer, she shoved in socks, underwear, and my backpack of school supplies. All my homework was ruined.

"NO!" Mother groaned, then took off for the laundry room.

"N-N-Not mine!" I yelped as I followed behind.

"Yep," Marnie quipped as she entered the laundry room.

To our dismay, the hamper sat empty.

"Mamma, you're busy and always complaining about laundry and chores. You complain a lot. I mean, like... All. The. Time. So, I decided to help out."

"What did you do?" Mother's eyeballs churned into bullseyes. "Where are my clothes? I had a pile of whites right here."

"In the dryer," Marnie declared, pleased with herself. "I got all your clothes, Mitzy's gross grandma underwear, and Dad's uniform in the same load. They all fit; isn't that amazing? I was going to surprise you but--"

"But my, my, my Bella Dahl blouse was in there. And my lingerie. On NO, I think my favorite smock was in that pile!!!!"

Mother's hand trembled as she reached for the dryer handle. "Please, Lord, let there be a miracle; let them be okay."

The dryer opened, and everything looked fine. Item by item, Mother, Marnie, and I folded and hung laundry.

"Well," Mother exhaled once the task was complete, "that's a relief. I was worried. For now on," Mother decreed as she collected her clothes, "the laundry room's off-limits in this house."

"Okay," Marnie chimed, "but what about dinner?"

"What do you mean?" Mother gasped.

"I saw the chicken in the refrigerator, so I threw it into the pressure cooker with…"

Mother took off towards the kitchen. As soon as she was out of sight, I leaned towards Marnie and asked, "Where'd you put them?"

"Put what?" she replied coyly.

"All Mother's clothes you ruined."

"In the Andrews' trash."

"What about my stuff?"

"What happened to them is actually an improvement. They're in your dresser."

"What about Dad's uniform?"

"Dad got called in and had to leave in a hurry. He didn't notice it when he got dressed, but when he ran out the door to get in his truck, it kind of glowed."

"What glowed?"

"His uniform," Marnie stated matter-of-factly.

"What do you mean by *glowed*?"

"Don't know how to explain it, but as soon as Dad ventured into the sunlight, his jumpsuit illuminated rainbows of color! I think it was from the fluorescent markers that got busted. It looked really cool."

"Gosh, I hope no one at the prison notices."

"Yeah, that might be a problem."

39

SATURDAY
NIGHT LIVE

March 1998

Halfway through my tenth-grade year, Rock Pudding appeared as the musical guest on *Saturday Night Live*. *SNL*, can you believe it!?! Here I was, this geeky, insecure high school reject one day, and the next, I had a first-class seat to New York City! *SNL* was our first big gig; all of us brimmed with expectations. New York City, I couldn't imagine a bigger change from my small, snuggly (and sometimes headachy) hometown of Bakersfield, California.

My inkling to urinate before walking on stage transitioned from Hurricane Gail Force 5 to an average rainstorm. Most importantly, I'd mastered avoiding the limelight for anything but singing. In other words, I kept my mouth shut. Whenever we interviewed at this place or that, I didn't do the speaking. I *never* did the speaking.

I wish I could blame my mother for this. I wish I could point my finger at Mac Michaels or some imaginary tyrant who'd taken control. But I can't. It was my own choice to avoid communicating in public. I chose to refuse interviews by directing media attention to Chris, Billy, or the guys. Before we even made it big, I decided my stutter would sabotage our success. I decided it was best to return to remaining mute because I didn't want my speech disorder to define the group.

If I could go back to her and change things, I would. I'd sit at the back table at a library (surrounded by books, so I felt safe). I'd explain to myself I wasn't the only person in the world with a stutter. I'd illuminate the fact that tens, perhaps thousands of others, have difficulty articulating language. Heck, I'd school myself into realizing that a speech disorder is only a tiny fraction of the issues people are born with (or acquire) wherein they perceive themselves as different. I get mad when I think about it because I could have inspired so many people at the time, people who needed inspiration. People who would have liked to see me overcome my stutter and succeed. Instead, I opted to hide it from the world. And by doing so, I let a lot of people down. Especially myself.

*　　*　　*

Rock Pudding had meetings with *SNL*'s producers, directors, and crewmembers. We had stage and music rehearsals — yes, we played live and not on a track. Most importantly, I met the host for that week's broadcast. (*SNL* has a different weekly host, usually a famous athlete, musician, actor/actress, comedian, or politician.) Anyhow, that week's host was none other than Tommy Townsend. *The* Tommy Townsend. Tommy Townsend, the seventeen-year-old heartthrob, starred in three movies and was slated to be the next up-and-coming star. The only thing better than Tommy Townsend's talent and grace was his smile. Tommy Townsend had a megawatt grin that ignited hearts worldwide. If I didn't have a secret crush on bad Billy Bearheart, meeting Tommy Townsend might have electrocuted my nerves.

*　　*　　*

"Holy moly!" Tommy walked in, wearing a fitted tee that accentuated his biceps. "You're Mitzy McGee!!! Man, I love Rock Pudding. You guys are killing it."

How did he recognize me? I'm wearing glasses and don't have a wig!

"Fancy meeting you here, although I already knew you'd be here. When they asked me to host, I may have kinda told them you're my favorite band."

Don't talk! He's cute, so cute, but don't let him hear your stutter!

"Hum-um," I half-smiled.

"Can't wait till your album's released. You guys are fantastic; I mean it. You've got a kind of talent I haven't heard in a while. You're like a sunflower in a world of thorns. My brother's your number one fan. He practically lives in your tee."

"Hum-um." I nodded affirmatively.

"Wow, I can't believe I'm meeting you."

You can't believe you're meeting me? It's just me. I'm a nobody. I'm a super-geek nobody.

"Enough about me, what about you? How do you like it here? How do you like New York? Man, I bet it's different from California!"

I smiled and shook my head again.

"Oh, I get it!" He smiled back. "You're saving your chops for rehearsal. I hear it's what a lot of singers do. That's smart. The way you slay a song is incredible; I bet it takes a lot out of—"

"Tommy," a stage manager summoned, "you're needed on set!"

There was an awkward pause.

"Now!" The man impatiently tapped his watch. "They're waiting!"

"Sorry, Mitz. Gotta go!" And then he rushed down the corridor towards Stage 1.

OMG! He's so good-looking, so gorgeous. He's nice and seems humble. Maybe I can trust him. Maybe I can trust him not to crush my heart.

* * *

Thursday, we ran into each other in the studio cafeteria.

"Man, look at this food!" Tommy announced as he loaded his plate. "They have everything."

Do it! You can say something. Try and say something. But I didn't. Instead, I gave him my shyest grin.

"There it is," Tommy chimed as he slid into a seat at a nearby table. "There's that pretty pout that's got my heart shipwrecked. There's something about you that's genuine. You aren't like anyone I've met. Something about you seems real."

I'm not real. There's little real about me. When I sing, I hide in a wig and eyeliner. I avoid the press and any form of public speaking because I have a stutter that I don't want anyone to hear. And I'm not going to talk to you even though I think you're totally hot and a great actor.

I grabbed a sandwich and turned to leave.

Tommy looked sad. "Geeze, I thought we'd..."

I'd almost reached the door when Tommy called, "Wait!" He jumped from his seat and dashed over. "I wanted to know if you'd like to go for a stroll after tomorrow's rehearsal, just for an hour. Your dad or brother can come if it's a problem. We'll get some ice cream and maybe ride around in a..."

Go! Go now!

And then the worst possible thing happened. My heart hijacked my head. Instead of bolting through the doorway and making a wild gallant dash to the safety of our trailer (where Richard and the guys waited), I stood there for a second, looked Tommy Townsend (fricken Tommy Townsend) in the eye, and smiled. I smiled at Tommy Townsend! And then I did the worst thing imaginable. Never in a million years would I believe it if my heart hadn't done such a wild, spontaneous thing.

I said, "Y-Y-Yeah, cool."

Then I bolted!

*   *   *

Friday's rehearsal sucked. I was so engrossed with the upcoming date with Tommy Townsend (if that was a date) that I couldn't put three notes together, let alone an entire song. I felt terrible for the guys because they never complained.

"C'mon, Mitz, you can do it." "We got faith in you, Mitz." "Don't worry, Mitz, we got your back." "We're in this together."

After rehearsal, I spotted a horse and carriage by the entrance as we left the studio.

"Man-oh-man, look at that!" 2-Tall pointed out the coachman in a fancy suit and the half dozen containers of sunflowers that lined the curb. "Someone went all out!"

"That's a class move," Chris decreed.

"You got that right," Billy agreed.

Oh, my gosh. I think that's for me. I think...

And then I read the placard in the driver's hand inscribed: *PICKUP FOR MITZY MCGEE.*

What do I do? What do I do?

Richard must have seen the placard. "Is that for you? Do you think the studio—"

"N-n-n-n-nope." My pace quickened. "Pretty sure they got the-the-the w-wrong person."

I rushed out of there as soon as I could.

* * *

Saturday night, I felt horrible during the 8:00 p.m. dress rehearsal. My singing sank to a new low. But after some fatherly encouragement from Richard, Rock Pudding killed the taped performance. I let them have a little grit and growl, and by the time the song ended, I blew it out of the park with Miss Mayme-inspired flair. We did a great job as Rock Pudding slayed "Millennial Girl" and had the time of our lives.

Between our performances, I watched a couple of skits starring Tommy Townsend.

Man, he's good. I hope he doesn't hate me for standing him up. That carriage ride looked incredible, and I love ice cream and flowers. It would have been spectacular. It would have been the perfect first date.

We sang "American Heroes like Leiann" for our second number because the producer specifically requested it. We had another great time. I bellowed that thing to the moon and back in another out-of-this-world performance.

Then – as happens on *SNL* – the cast members and comedians ventured onto the stage as the host bid everyone a good night. But this time, something happened. Something unusual. Something different and unusual.

When Tommy Townsend returned to the stage, the lighting suddenly went dim while the musical accompanist paused. Everyone became quiet, even the audience silenced to a still. For a second, I thought he'd announce what I had done to the world. He'd tell them I stood him up on a carriage ride without explanation or reason. The quieter it got, the louder my heart screamed.

That is when the most amazing, horrific, surprising, astronomical thing that could have possibly happened — happened. Something none of us expected. Something I never imagined in my wildest dreams. The spotlight traveled off stage and slowly panned through the audience to a young female marine in the front row. That's when I recognized her. That's when I recognized my sister! Leiann was there! My sister was there! I hadn't seen her since she left for the military. I couldn't believe it!

I couldn't control myself. One second, I was on stage with all these famous people (and the world) watching me, and the next, I took flight into the audience. I ran to her as fast as I could. We hugged! I hugged my sister! I hugged Leiann! And then, I started bawling. Then Jimmy Jay was there, then the guys. We were all so happy, so extremely happy. It was a celebration where time whisked us away to a magical place where it was just us.

Somewhere else, somewhere far off in the distance, I heard Tommy Townsend close out the show. "*SNL* would like to thank Lance Corporal McGee and the fine American heroes who sacrifice themselves and serve our country. It doesn't get better than this, folks. Good night."

It wasn't until our flight back to Bakersfield that my mind pieced things together. Tommy's words drifted into my mind as I gazed upon a graceful patchwork of farms, homes, lakes, and trees. "Man, I love Rock Pudding; you guys are killing it." "When they asked me to host the show, I may have kinda told the producer you were my favorite band." "My brother wears your tee shirt all the time."

That's when I realized Tommy Townsend arranged the whole thing. We weren't famous. We were a nobody band destined to be a one-hit-wonder. I knew it felt odd *SNL* wanted us to perform. We never would have been flown to New York if it wasn't for Tommy Townsend. And then it dawned on me that Tommy probably arranged for us to play "American Heroes like Leiann" because he wanted to create that moment. Everything that happened to us in New York – *SNL*, tickets to a Broadway show, the pizzas delivered to our room, and spending time with Leiann – had all been arranged by Tommy.

40

THE WEREWOLF OF BAKERSFIELD

Summer 1998

That summer, Mother's Venus Boutique and Day Spa had a steady stream of customers. Marnie decided to save the planet by picking up trash while I (thinking of you-know-who) created the lyrics for "Shipwrecked." Words flowed onto the page as if from a daze. I wasn't stuck on the guy. Heck, I didn't even know if I liked Tommy Townsend and his silly boyish grin. All I know is that Shipwrecked immediately became another hit.

For our first video, "American Heroes like Leiann," our producer recorded us in a studio, splicing in clips of soldiers making it home to joyous receptions. To make it personal, he included coverage of our appearance on *SNL*. That video ended up being a theme song for family reunions, an acknowledgment of military personnel's service to our country, and a tear-jerker rolled into one. It garnered a lot of publicity and our first nomination for the MTV Music Awards.

For "Shipwrecked," our producer had us don zoo animal costumes as we mocked skydiving out of a plane, except Chris Lee's parachute doesn't open, and he plummets to his peril. That's the whole song: us floating through the air as we fall to the ground. None of us quite got why he wanted us to fall through the air for a song titled "Shipwrecked." Nevertheless, the imagery and special effects earned another nomination for the infamous award show.

When we taped "Skateboarders Anthem," I saw the cute skater wear and felt razzed that I'd look like a normal person in a video. Then the producer explained that while I performed tricks on a skateboard (with the aid of a stunt double), I'd sprout arm and facial hair as I transformed into a werewolf. At the end of the video, I howled my approval for skaters' rights. I, personally, thought the concept was strange. However, Billy and the boys kept pushing me to do it. Before long, I was in makeup in various stages of hairiness. Little did I know, skaters and non-skaters would howl their approval for years.

As for "Millennial Girl," I wore a boxing costume and sometimes brandished gloves. Of all the videos made that summer, I liked that one the most because I wasn't turning into a hairy beast, wrapped like a mummy, falling through the air like a flailing hippopotamus.

All in all, writing songs was fun. Making the videos was fun. Practicing and playing with the band was fun. Everything was great until I realized if any of our nominations won an MTV Video Music Award, I'd have to go on stage and make a speech in front of hundreds of spectators and millions of viewers worldwide.

41

MTV VIDEO MUSIC AWARDS

August 30, 1998

T he MTV Video Music Awards (*VMAs*) is a once-a-year spectacle honoring the best in music videos. There are awards, performances, and crazy antics. And there's a lot of raving about this and that. Basically, it's the Oscars for us musicians. Except instead of sitting in our seats and observing the show, musicians schmooze as they vie for who's-who in entertainment. That's the part I dreaded the most. I dreaded the schmoozing. And I especially dreaded walking out on stage and presenting the award for top new artist. And who do you think the head honchos at MTV selected to accompany me to the microphone and present the award? That's right: it was none other than Tommy Townsend. Fricken Tommy Townsend, the up-and-coming shoo-in for an Oscar. The entire drive to Los Angeles, my stomach wrenched into so many knots, I think it knitted a sweater.

Luckily, I had my family and my band family. We drove in a caravan of cars and trucks, arriving in plenty of time to warm up for "Millennial Girl" and "Killer Valentine Vixen."

For the VMA's, we decided to keep our style simple by wearing all black with wide-brimmed ball caps and dark glasses. *That* I loved; it was a tremendous change from all the crazy costumes I got stuck wearing in videos. I opted to wear tights under a mini, sneakers, and a cropped tee (all black, of course). To give my shirt a little pop, Marnie bedazzled a heart on the bodice. The only thing that wasn't black was the fuchsia wig I borrowed from Miss Ruby.

* * *

As I waited in an alcove backstage, scared to death about the announcement with Tommy, Marnie found me in a midstate of panic.

"Mitzy," my sister worried, "are you okay?"

"I th-th-think I-I-I-I'm gonna be-be sick."

"You can do it, I swear. If you can pretend to fall out of a plane. If you can sprout German Shepard legs and arm hair in front of the world. If you can sing in front of eleven million people, you can say those eleven words."

Eleven words was my part of the skit with Tommy Townsend, introducing finalists for the New Artist Award.

"Are you more nervous about Tommy or making the announcement?"

I couldn't say; I didn't know myself. I tried my best not to barf or pee on myself.

"I'm sure you'll do fine."

"I can't do this," I gushed defeatedly. "I can't g-g-get up there and-and make a speech."

She let out a dramatic exhale, and then she leaned in and whispered, "I'll do it."

"W-What!?!"

"We look alike. We're about the same height and have the same features. No one will know."

My heart jumpstarted. It sounded like a lame-brained idea, but it had my mind whirling with intrigue.

"We'll exchange clothes. With the hat, wig, and sunglasses, no one can see your face anyway. I'll go up on stage, do the presentation with Tommy, and return in plenty of time to trade back so you can make your performance." She grabbed hold of my hand. "But we only do it this one time."

Now, I'd be lying if I didn't say I wasn't worried about Marnie's scheme. It was a foolish, crazy, lame-brained idea that could have gotten us into trouble. However, the moment those words left her lips, my storm of anxiety shrank to a molehill. A doable molehill. A molehill that made the *VMAs* festive and fun.

* * *

"Hey, you' all," she greeted. Marnie looked good; she had my blacked-out clothes, Miss Ruby's wig, the ball cap (turned to the side), and sunglasses. She looked like a teenage rock star.

"Hey to you," Tommy smiled at Marnie, "and good evening to everyone, including those watching from their living rooms and couches worldwide."

"Speaking of the world," Marnie cut him off.

Wait a minute!?! I fretted as I watched from a monitor in the dressing room. *That's not in the skit. What's she doing?*

"Okay, yeah," Tommy went with the flow.

"Well, I just want everyone to pitch in and take better care of our planet.

"That's admirable," Tommy chuckled. And then he paused, smiled assuredly, and asked, "Anything else?"

"Yeah, pick up your trash, peoples, and watch your emissions. We only have one planet. We gotta take care of our world, or—"

"Ladies and gentlemen," Tommy flashed his roguish grin, "apparently, Mitzy McGee is as passionate about saving the world as she is about music."

The audience chuckled.

"That's an admirable quality, but let's get on with..."

* * *

What's she doing!?! I fretted. Thirty-five minutes after the new artist nomination with Tommy, Marnie still hadn't returned to the room. *I have to perform in—*

The door flew open, and Marnie rushed in, bubbling with excitement. "Sorry it took so long," she huffed, "but I gave some interviews."

"You w-w-w-what!?!"

The two of us unzipped our clothes, preparing to change back.

"It's nothing," she vetted. "Just hurry and get out there. The band's waiting. By the way, everyone loves Rock Pudding, and--"

"A-A-A-And what?"

"And Tommy Townsend knew it wasn't you."

"*WHAT*!?!"

"Yeah, I thought I pulled it off, but as I headed back, he called me over."

"What'd he s-s-s-s-say?"

"He just said to tell you he says 'hi.'"

"That's it?"

"Yep." She angled my cap to the side. "Now, go out there and give 'em gravel. Give 'em grit. Give 'em an entire meal with the fries, some nuggets, a hamburger, and a shake."

I laughed, and then I hugged her.

"What's so funny?"

"You, silly. I-I-I-I think you might be hungry."

42

ELEVENTH GRADE

September 1998

E leventh grade began as some sort of sci-fi time warp. When I ventured onto the campus, crowds of fans pointed me out as star-struck groupies. They wore Rock Pudding tees and followed me, requesting autographs and merchandise. I tried to ignore them, but they followed me into the restroom, clustered around my stall, and awaited the sound of my urination. I couldn't pee like that, not with that kind of pressure. So, five minutes after walking into school, I feigned being sick and went home.

That pretty much ended my experience at Stockdale. I took the GED and passed. I wanted to enroll in correspondence school but got busy shooting videos. That year, we shot a lot of videos. Unfortunately, one of our videos had to be shelved due to technical difficulties.

When we shot "Breaking Benjamin Pane," we thought everything went well. Unfortunately, we realized the camera angles had been off when we saw the completed footage. Basically, we had two and a half hours of butt shots. Not good butt shots. They were embarrassing and outright gross. Instead of firing the director, we set the video aside and got to work on our next project. By then, we already had a dozen videos circuiting television, while one of our songs seemed to play every few minutes on the radio.

* * *

Mac Michaels hadn't selected a specific date; however, the groundwork had been laid for our tour. Until then, we spent most of our time working on songs and performances. All the while, we had a steady stream of media interviews. The interviews, that's where Mac wasn't happy.

"I don't like it!" He seethed once he saw Marnie in my wig again. "It's wrong. It's deceptive. If someone finds out you're doing this. If this gets out, it could be the end of Rock Pudding. Heck, it could be the end of me. I've invested a lot in this band. Something like this could topple me. It could ruin my reputation. I just don't—"

"D-D-Don't worry," I soothed as Marnie walked up to the microphone on the set of *Good Morning America*. "No one will f-f-f-f-find out."

"This is the last time." He shook his head, determined. "This has to stop!"

"Okay," I replied, even though we both knew I was lying.

There's NO WAY I will give an interview or make a speech. Besides, Marnie's good at it. She's funny and witty and has them eating out of her hand.

I watched as she gabbed with the broadcasters.

Look how they love her. Remember all the good stuff that's been said. Marnie isn't ruining anything. She's making the band great!

And even though I wasn't true to my word (Marnie made the next thirty to forty interviews, parades, meet and greets, and talk show appearances), Mac was true to his. On March 4th – two days after 2-Talls' twenty-first birthday – Rock Pudding joined Stallion Brigade and Shamrock Sky Stompers as we set out on a multi-city, multi-million-dollar world tour.

* * *

Mother indicated she would fly out and meet us around the end of the summer. Richard, on the other hand, arranged to swap shifts (trade jobs) so he'd be there every other weekend of our tour. Marnie and I couldn't travel the world alone, so Mrs. Dunlop (Marnie's childhood babysitter) agreed to chaperone.

The night before we left for Tokyo, my heart filled with sadness and gloom. *I'm going to miss this place. I'm going to miss the bathrooms, the food, the fights, and Richard's corny correctional jargon. This place changed me; I'm going to miss every part of my life here. Somehow, this room became my haven from the craziness in the world. I felt safe here. I felt protected. It's as though Sarah McGee's been by my side every step of the way. I feel as though her mural cradled me in a space where I felt safe, sheltered, and loved.*

SECTION V

AGES NINETEEN TO TWENTY-ONE

43

AFTERMATH OF REGRET

February 2001

"What have you-you done!?!" I gasped. Rock Pudding was in London, performing at the Royal Variety Show, when I learned Marnie accepted Mitzy McGee's invitation to tea with the Queen.

"She likes my mission of saving the planet, so I accepted." Marnie shrugged. "Not going to insult the Queen of England and say 'no' — that would be rude. That could cause an international relations crisis. That could put Rock Pudding on the map as bad news. That could—"

"Okay. Gosh, I-I just w-w-w-wish—"

"What?" Marnie challenged. "That we stopped a long time ago. That we never switched places at the *VMA*'s. That you didn't have me do an acne commercial with humongous pimples on my face or the one where I act like a constipated snob because I drive the wrong car? Yeah, me too."

My eyes trailed to the ground.

"Sorry." She handed me her jeans to put on. "I appreciate the opportunity of meeting all these famous people and getting the chance to promote a healthy planet, but this has gotten old. I'm tired of being Marnie-mouth. I feel we're on a runaway train, and around any corner, we'll derail."

"I know. Hiding my stutter meant everything to-to-to me, but now—"

"Now, you feel like a traitor."

"Y-Y-Y—"

"Now, you've botched anything to do with an unmentioned Hollywood heartthrob?"

"Y-Y-Y—"

"Now you've ruined your chance of supporting those with special needs or feel they are perceived as being different."

"Yes, b-b-but—"

"Listen, I love you, but I never thought it'd go this far. When we first switched places, it was because you were full mode panic attack." She scanned my eyes to ensure she didn't hurt my feelings. "But in the hundred or so times since, we've lost pieces of ourselves. I've shrunk to your shadow. I no longer have a life outside of being your mouth. But I went on. I continued this charade for you. Anytime you want to come clean, I'll be by your side. I'll take the blame, the negative attention, and the wrath. We can't go on like this forever. We've got to come clean and tell the world, or you and I will never reclaim our lives."

"I w-w-wish it could happen, but I'm n-n-n-not ready."

"Then I guess tomorrow it's tea and crumpets with the Queen. Hope she likes my idea of converting the palace to solar energy."

"Yeah," I grumbled.

And then my beautiful, loyal, and sometimes aggravating younger sister stepped out of the dressing room. As I pinned my wig in the aftermath of regret, I smacked on my game face and prepared for the show.

If I were to describe the three and a half years that led to the Queen's performance, I'd say it was a roller coaster of fantastical highs shadowed with remorse. Living a lie wasn't easy. Still, no matter how many times I wanted to come clean and let the world know about my stutter, I never mustered the courage to make things right. At that point in my life, I – Misty McGee, rock star stutterer extraordinaire – was a stereotypical mixed-up nineteen-year-old. After the applause – after the lights dimmed and the adoration of being a star quieted to a simmer – I drowned in my pit of self-loathing.

44

THREE LITTLE WORDS

Summer 2001

My feet hurt. My head hurt. My throat had an irritating case of scratches, and I was mad dog tired as I headed up the 99 to Bakersfield. All I wanted was a few days of peace and quiet (and some of Richard's barbeque) before Rock Pudding set out on another stint of performances. But once I opened the door, my world flipped upside down. The house had been transformed. Everything I loved was gone!

"What happened?" I gasped. "W-W-Where's all-all-all-all—"

"Hello, darling," Mother greeted. "Oh, I had a yard sale and sold all that stuff. Whatever I couldn't get rid of, I donated to the Goodwill or tossed in the trash."

Sarah McGee's trinkets and charm had been banished from every room. What remained was the cold-hearted lair of a department store.

"I got new furniture and decorations. Isn't it nice!"

"But-but-but-but-but—"

"Oh, that old clutter just collected dust; it—"

"But that-that-that was Sarah's s-s-s—"

"Mitzy, darling, that woman's been gone for many years. I've endured living here for a long time with all her ghosts. It was time. Time to take the shrine down and..."

I rushed to the side of the house, took a deep breath, and lifted the lid from the trash bin.

"Mitzy!" Mother followed me. "What are you doing? It's trash! Why are you digging in the garbage?"

"Where's the p-p-p-porcelain pony?"

"Porcelain, *what?*"

"Sarah's porcelain pony from the mantel. It means a-a-a lot to Jimmy Jay. Did you get r-r-rid of it without even asking? How-how-how could you?"

The trash bin contained nothing but food scraps and crumpled wrapers.

"Mitzy, darling, that stuff went out weeks ago. And you shouldn't be mad at me; Richard said it was okay. He gave me—"

And then I turned and faced this woman. This woman who was my mother all my life. This woman who had said and done so many hurtful things. And I finally said the three words the little girl in my heart had always yearned for.

"I-I-I hate you," I growled. Then I stormed through the doorway and left.

45

RHINESTONE-STUDDED LIE

2002

The next year or so was a fanfare of festivals, concerts, appearances, and another round of performances at the VMA's. Nothing felt better than standing in front of an audience and belting notes with Miss Mayme Tucker's flair. I still experienced bouts of anxiety before I ventured on stage, but all of that disappeared when I lost myself in song.

Singing like that was a dream. Not going to lie here; becoming a rock star was pretty amazing. Yeah, Mac Michaels had me in some ridiculous videos, such as the time I wandered the desert in bedazzled disco attire and a beekeeper's mask. And some of my costumes were outright bizarre. Why would any sane video director have me wear an astronaut suit with rhinestone heels?

Nevertheless, being in the moment at concerts felt as though I'd grown wings and soared above the hills and the trees. When I sang, I forgot I was a geeky girl with a stutter. I forgot about the dilemma with my lie. When the song ended and I walked off stage, the flight of a free bird transitioned back to reality. That's when I returned to being a disgruntled liar with underlying friction with her mom.

Sometimes, she tried, but my mother had never been the best mother. That should have been apparent within the first few pages of this journal. But I always had hope for her. I hoped she'd become the mother of my dreams. I hoped she'd become my imaginary version of Sarah McGee.

"Give her some time," Richard always said. "Your mother's been through a lot. Just give her time, and she'll come around. You two will make amends; I'm sure of it."

I wasn't sure of it, though. I didn't think it was possible. Nevertheless, the more I distanced myself from my mom, the more I wondered about other relatives. Mainly, I wondered about my father's side of the family. Not Richard, I'm talking about the mysterious and prominent Lou Thomas Greenshield.

46

JAILBIRDS

Spring 2003

After a successful stint of concerts, we stopped in Italy, where we dined at a table at the Hotel Londra Palace in Venice, which overlooked the famed Grand Canal. And it was there – after a lip-smacking feast of a lifetime – that Billy Bearheart not so spontaneously rose from his seat.

"Okay, okay," he tapped his glass with his spoon, "can I have your attention? Everyone quiet down. I have something to announce."

Jaslene's expression warmed with curiosity.

"I just want to proclaim my love for this crazy, insanely beautiful woman of mine, and..." Billy reached into his pocket and retrieved a small velvet box.

"Whoa!" Jimmy Jay grunted. "Holy moly, I think he's gonna do it!"

Jaslene glared at Jimmy Jay.

"Shhh," Chris Lee heeded.

Everyone went silent. The other patrons were quiet. The (cameriere) waiters and cameriera (waitresses) were quiet. Even the merchants along the riverwalk seemed to become soundless. Well, except Jimmy Jay, who nonchalantly crunched on a breadstick.

"Jaslene," Billy knelt before her with a ring in his hand, "my baby, my love, my better half—"

"You got that right!" 2-Tall cut in.

"Since we met, you've made me the happiest man in the world, and I'd..."

What on earth? He's proposing? I can't believe it; he's so young. What is he now? Twenty-three? Four? Five? Twenty-five's too young to... Wait, he's doing it! Billy's proposing to Jaslene. I never saw this happening, not in a million years. I mean, I kind of saw it happening because they're together and all, but, but, but...

Much of that night draws a blur. Jaslene was nice and all (actually, she was terrific), but I never expected a proposal. I just remember between the platters of lasagna, linguini, and these really good cheese-mushroom thingies, I realized I had to let go of my childhood crush on bad Billy Bearheart. He was my bandmate and brother, and they were genuinely good together.

Someday, I vowed, *I'll find a love of my own. Someone as good as my dad (Richard) and good-looking as Billy. Someone loyal and trustworthy. Someone who will love me for me.*

*   *   *

Billy and Jaslene married at a secluded estate in Maui. The beach was beautiful. The weather was beautiful. Jaslene was beautiful, and Billy was particularly stunning as they wed under the haloing hues of a tangerine sunset. The only people present at this exclusive, top-secret event (the only people invited) were a hundred and twenty of our closest friends and family members. And a half dozen paparazzi. And the dozens of journalists who viewed the spectacle from vessels and boats nearby, taking photos and a live video feed. Oh, and the helicopter that hovered overhead.

Yep, Billy's wedding was billed as an "exclusive, private, top-secret event" even though he hand-selected an army of photographers and photojournalists. That's a bizarre concept with fame. Famous people pretend to be exclusive while reaping the rewards of publicity and the sweet, succulent benefit of free lodging, food, fancy cars, and designer wedding gowns.

So, it was at the reception of this "exclusive, private, top-secret event" that everything went haywire. That's the day I ruined the wedding of my buddy and bandmate. That's the day I got half the wedding party thrown in the slammer. It started with a simple, old-fashioned ceremony of cutting the cake.

* * *

As I (the maid of honor) smiled by the cake table in marquise emerald earrings and a Versace gown, Jaslene - in a twenty-seven-thousand-dollar Valentino gown she graciously agreed to wear for free - posed, holding a silver serving spatula. She looked stunning. I mean it; I don't think I've ever seen a more beautiful bride.

Anyhow, the moment wasn't exactly spontaneous. Instead of slicing into the cake, we remained statues as four or five photographers clustered around the table, trying to take the perfect picture. And it was then – as my fake smile started to hurt, as Jaslene giggled in fits, as Billy tried to sneak in another kiss, and as Jimmy Jay let out an obnoxious and rather loud belch – that "it" happened. It being the unraveling of two events at the same time: the ruin of their reception and the obliteration of my lie.

"So, Billy," the paparazzi with bristled eyebrows snidely called out, "is it true your singer, here, Mitzy McGee..." He pointed to me. "... is a fake and a liar, and Rock Pudding's covering up for a—"

"What!" Billy snapped. "Dude, you've gotta stop."

"Security," Jaslene summoned, "get him out of here!"

"What'd you say about my sister!?!" Jimmy Jay boomed as he reared from his seat.

No! No! No! My mind raced.

"Is it true?" the paparazzi pressed. "She can't talk, right? Is it true she has a stutter, and all your records are a lie? Is it—"

With zero warning whatsoever, Jaslene delicately lifted the top tier from the stack, brought it back, and threw it at the paparazzi's head with so much velocity it caused him to backstep, slip, and inadvertently fall. Billy, Chris Lee, and 2-Tall rushed to the table. Instead of beating the you-know-what out of the guy, they scooped handfuls of cake and hurled it at him. Then Marnie dragged a trash can (filled with leftovers from dinner), lifted it with Jimmy Jay's assistance, and buried the guy in a deluge of food slop. A couple of his paparazzi friends dashed over to stop us. But it was too late; the elegant, highfalutin affair turned into a down-and-dirty food fight. And the entire time we hurled food and got covered in glop, paparazzi photographers snapped pics.

An hour and forty-three minutes later, we waited in the small, cramped quarters of the local police substation for Mac Michaels to bail us out. We were covered in food and feeling remorseful. And it was then – as I felt terrible for my part in inciting the melee that ruined Jaslene's and Billy's reception, as I felt sick to my stomach because my lie jeopardized the future of the band, and as I felt like it was the end of the world because I knew nothing would ever be the same – that's when it happened. That's when the stars and heavens shifted alignment, and everything important became right.

"I-I-I-I'm sorry," I whispered to Jaslene, who sat beside me on a bench in our cell in her food-saturated Valentino gown.

"For what?" Her hair had icing blobs as she reached over and clasped my hand.

Tears fell from my eyes. "Because I ruined your reception. I-I-I—"

"*That* wasn't you!" she assured. "HE did it. That-that backstab-bing, bushy eye-browed, good for nothing, idiot shouldn't have—"

"It's my l-l-l-lie that did that. I-I-I'm s-s-so—"

"Mitz," Jaslene's voice softened, "this dress… The fancy wedding… Cutting a cake… Everything – all the pomp and circumstance of the ceremony – means nothing compared to our friendship."

"Huh?"

"You Mitz!" She smiled. "You mean more to me than some silly ceremony. Or dress. Or going to jail. And I know Billy feels the same. Girl, I know you've got a big ole barricade around your heart. I know when you were small, you were bullied. I know you invented this crazy lie because you're uncomfortable with yourself. But I see you, the real you, and I love you for who you are. Your stutter is nothing to be ashamed of because it's a part of you. If you could just see yourself from my eyes, you'd see how truly great you are."

"Why w-w-w-would you say that?"

"Because," she chuckled as she squeezed my fingers, "I'm your friend, and that's what friends do. I'll always have your back, Mitz. Through thick and thin, through the turmoil of getting arrested and thrown in a cruddy jail cell on my wedding day, and even when you don't use your best judgment."

I wanted to talk but found it hard to breathe. This wallow in my throat absorbed all my energy. I couldn't understand being loved like that. I had girls who were my friends, but not like that. Not loyal. No one who vowed to support me through "thick and thin." No one promised to stand by me when I messed up. It was a little much; I couldn't talk as tears rained down my cheeks.

And it was then, in that cell, on that day, that the little girl in me who had always wanted a best friend – a true and real best friend – had all her hopes and dreams come true. All I could do was sit there and cry as the two of us sat in a musty chamber, covered in cake and an assortment of smelly food glops, happily holding hands.

*   *   *

Four days later, at Mac Michaels' mansion studio in Los Angeles, I vowed to make things right.

"I'm s-s-sorry for everything," I said to Mac and the band. "I'm ready to come clean. I'm ready to-to-to tell the truth and let the world know I have a s-s-s-stutter."

"Mitzy. Kid. Darling. Dollface," Mac decreed. "I've wanted that more than anything. I've wanted to hear those words since I met you. How many years has it been? What, seven and a half years now?"

I shook my head as I looked down.

"But now isn't the best time. That zany wedding fiasco put you back on the top of the charts. I got every radio station blowing up the lines, wanting to hear your next album. I got everyone and their brother wanting to tour with you. I got endorsements from here to Timbuctoo."

I stood speechless.

"They just called from the Glastonbury Festival. They want you there like now. Later today, you're hopping on a flight to Europe. Tomorrow, you perform in front of 160,000 people. This will be your largest live performance yet. And now I've got calls from Hong Kong, Australia, Japan, Sweden... Shoot, I've had so many calls I can't keep track. That little stunt of yours made you the hottest name in entertainment in the world. Everyone wants you."

"What about that reporter?" Chris Lee cut in.

"Paid him off. He's forty thousand dollars richer and a happy camper. We won't hear a thing from him."

"Good," 2-Tall spouted, "because I don't want anyone giving our girl any more grief."

47

THE CALL

June 4, 2004

An innocent call set off the next twist of events. In the limo on the way to the airport – as occupants in passing cars called out, "I love you!!!" "Rock & Roll!" "Rock Pudding's my favorite band!" – I decided to phone Lou Greenshield. It wasn't planned, although I had daydreamed about it for years. His secretary patched me through without question.

"Mitzy," he greeted in an edged tone.

Lou Greenshield said my name. He actually said my name!

"I-I-I-I'm your g-g-granddaughter. I-I-I-I'm heading to-to Europe for-for—"

"Yeah, saw it on the news. We maintain tabs on your whereabouts."

He follows me! Lou Greenshield cares about me!

My thoughts swarmed as hope welled in my bones. There was an awkward silence where neither of us said anything for a moment.

"Then-then-then can I ask why you've never contacted me or-or-or called? Why haven't—"

"Don't play coy with me."

What does he mean?

"You were supposed to stick to the agreement."

"Agreement? W-W-What a-a--"

"The no-contact agreement. As the attorney general for the state, I don't want my name and reputation tarnished by being associated with someone such as yourself."

"What?"

"You! Everything about you could tarnish my--"

"Are y-y-you talking about my stutter?"

"Moldy Pudding, or whatever you call yourself, I made a deal with that loser mother of yours that if I helped her hapless husband when he was in a jam, all of this would go away."

"What?"

"You. You were to stay out of my life. You can tell your mother the deal's off now that you've broken the agreement. Time to reap what you sow, young lady. Time to pay."

My stomach sank. I had no idea what he meant. *What did my mother do to Lou Greenshield? Why does he hate her so? Why does she have so many secrets?*

* * *

Lou Greenshield evaporated from my mind when Rock Pudding took stage at The Glastonbury Festival in Pilton, England. The Glastonbury Festival, one of the world's biggest music venues, had a reputation of skyrocketing stars to fame. And even though I had a lot going on in my mind, Rock Pudding had a stellar performance.

As I sang for the zillionth time – belting my heart out while hamming it up with dance moves and poses – I got to a place where being on stage had become an addiction. On stage, I bathed in the audience's admiration. I felt included, and it filled my soul with joy.

The moment I walked off stage, that joy was stolen when a stagehand shoved a phone in my hand, stating the caller said it was urgent.

"Hello?" I greeted, feeling perturbed.

"Mitzy, get out!" my mother huffed.

Listen to the way she speaks to me. She didn't even say hello. She hasn't talked to me in – what – ages, and when she does, it's her usual drama BS!

"W-W-What?" I retorted. I couldn't believe my mother would call like that.

"Greenshield called a press conference. He's accused you of extortion and theft."

My breath stuck. "WHAT!?!"

"He told the world about your stutter and said he has proof Rock Pudding's a fake."

"No!"

"People are angry. There's a bunch of lies going around. I think you might be in danger. You, Marnie, and the band need to get out of there. It's--"

Marnie and Jaslene rushed over.

"We gotta get," Marnie said. "The press just labeled Rock Pudding a fraud. They say we lip-synched everything. That we're a bunch of posers who duped the public out of millions. People are mad. Mac just got a death threat."

"Can't be that bad," Jimmy Jay grumbled as he reached over the veggie tray for a meatball sandwich.

That's when we saw three or four paparazzi rushing towards the stage, and by the glare and ghoul in their eyes, we knew our worst nightmare had come true. No one looked back as we weaved through backstage personnel to an awaiting taxi.

*   *   *

Someone spotted us as our SUV traversed the long scenic road to the airport. Instead of cheering positive affirmations of support, she yelled obscenities while her passenger chucked a soda can at our car. Our driver thought we were about to get robbed, so he sped up to make a getaway. Four or five vehicles pursued us in a chase with a couple of close calls where we almost crashed. Fortunately, our driver performed a sneaky (illegal) turn into the departure gate without anyone getting killed.

And it was while we waited in the airport lounge – as we sat incognito in hats and jackets purchased at the duty-free store – that we witnessed the wrath of negative publicity on a nearby television. The story was broadcast on every channel.

That's what I get for lying. That's what I get for lying. Lying is stupid. Why did I do it? My mother lies all the time, and I hate that about her. Why did I continue with the lie?

Story after story labeled us as a fraud. Making matters worse, fans from all over the world were pictured burning Rock Pudding gear.

"They're garbage," a fifteen-year-old spat, "everything they sang about is a lie."

*   *   *

Twenty-three hours. Just twenty-three hours. That's how much time it took for everything to unravel. Dozens of death threats were lobbed through phone messages, texts, Myspace, and the news. As we watched television in the limo that carted us to Mac Michaels' estate, we saw our most dependable fan (the founder and president of The Rock Pudding Fan Club) have a live feed of getting a tattoo cover-up. Her Millennial Girl inkblot transformed into a giant battleship encompassing the entire top left portion of her back. And that wasn't all. News stations from all around called our families and friends, trying to dig up as much as they could so they could cobble nails in our coffin.

*   *   *

"Basically," Mac Michaels explained at his house, "we're ruined. I don't see a way out of this. I mean, I've hired a top-notch public relations expert. She heads a company that's gotten a lot of high-ranking politicians out of hot water, including JFK, BC, and JB."

"What kind of hot water did JB get into?" 2-Tall cut in. "I never heard anything."

"Precisely," Mac snapped. "Her company's commingling research to develop a plan. She's due to arrive Wednesday around nine."

"Great," Jaslene said, "maybe she'll fix things."

"Yeah!" Jimmy Jay sat on a recliner with his long-tousled hair in a man bun. "Never give up hope. Something good could always happen."

"Man," 2-Tall speculated, "what are you all gonna do if this doesn't work out?"

"What do you mean?" Marnie asked.

"What's your Plan B?"

"I always wanted to be a dental hygienist," Marnie proclaimed. "I like teeth clean like I like our planet clean."

"Geeze," Jimmy Jay munched on a shrimp, "I never really thought about it. Guess I'd become a beach bum."

"Something with the clothes industry," Chris Lee proclaimed. "Maybe I'll start my own—"

"Stay home and raise kids," Billy cut him off. "Jaslene and I wanna have a big family."

Everyone chuckled because we already knew that. Billy and Jaslene were very much in love and ready to start a family.

"Are you trying to tell us something?" Marnie hinted.

"Not yet," Jaslene smiled, "but soon. What about you, Mitz?" My best friend looked at me with eyes that sparkled with assurance.

"I'll probably l-l-lock myself in a cabin somewhere and w-w-write novels."

"Nah," 2-Tall cut me off, "you'd miss us too much."

"Yeah," I smiled back, "I would."

* * *

Later that day, as we lingered around the Beverly Hills mansion/ estate game room, Mac rushed through the door, shouting, "You're not going to believe this!"

"What?" A couple of us responded at the same time.

Mac frantically searched for something. "Has anyone seen the remote control?" He toppled an end table and proceeded to toss cush-ions from a couch. "I need the controller! I need it now! We have an emergency—"

"Oh," Jimmy Jay leaned forward and retrieved it from beneath his right hip, "you mean this?"

Once Mac collected the controller, he directed it at the television that comprised an entire wall. The screen lit to an image no one expected. Not in a million years. Not in a million trillion zillion years. The image on the screen was my mom.

*   *   *

"I'm sorry," she began, "this…" She took a deep breath, adjusted her hair, and slowly raised her eyes to meet the camera. "I'm not good at this sort of thing."

"Just start by introducing yourself," an unidentified commentator jutted in. "People need to hear your name,"

"Oh, ah, sorry." She adjusted her hair again. She didn't need to change anything; she looked perfect. "Ummm…"

"What's she doing?" Jimmy Jay grumbled. "What's going on?"

"I'd like to start by telling you my name is Victoria McGee. It didn't use to be McGee. My maiden name is DeRienzo. I guess my story starts there."

"Can we get on with it?" the commentator cut in.

Mother's brows furrowed. "When I was seven, my parents went to jail for neglecting me. I don't know why they kept me chained to my bed; I wasn't a bad kid. But they did what they did. No one in my family wanted me, so the government put me in foster care."

What?

"And…" the commentator pressed.

"And that's where I grew up. I grew up in the system, passed around like a piece of garbage for years when I was finally taken into a good home. The home of Kim and Lou Greenshield, where I lived with their sons Harold and Eugene."

I never knew that. I never knew my mother was chained to a bed and then brought up in the system. That would be terrible. She's said so many lies; I never would have believed the truth.

"The Greenshield boys weren't nice. They did things that went ignored. Bad things. Really bad things that never should have happened. I tried to report them, but no one listened. No one *ever* listened."

"And," the commentator pressed again.

"When I was fifteen, I became pregnant. Kim and Lou didn't want their sons going to jail, so they sent me away to Bakersfield, where they put me up in an apartment. They had me lie about my age and the circumstances of the pregnancy by threatening to take away my baby. Eugene committed suicide later that year while Harold worked for his father, who went on to become the state attorney general."

No, Mother, no. I never imagined you went through that. It must have taken incredible strength to call Lou Greenshield that day to help Richard. You love Richard that much.

"The reason I'm telling you this is because that baby's in a heap of trouble now. And I want to make things right."

"Okay," the commentator grunted.

"I was a terrible mother. Heck, I was messed up from being passed around and all the abuse. I know that's not an excuse, but I admit I done bad things by that little girl."

"What is her name?"

"My daughter is Mitzy McGee..."

A gasp seeped from someone in the vicinity.

"... and the lie about her stutter is true. Mitzy has a stutter when she speaks, and her sister, Marnie, has covered for her in talk interviews, commercials, and television appearances."

"Why is she doing this?" Chris Lee speculated. "Is she selling us out for money? Is she getting a payout? I wonder how much she's getting paid to do this?"

Mother went on almost as if she knew what the world was thinking. "I'm not here for the money. I'm doing this because I want to come clean."

Mother blew her nose, and then her eyes panned into the camera.

"It's my fault. All of it is my fault. I forced my daughters to switch places. I masterminded the lie. It's not Mitzy's fault. No one is to blame here but me. The girls were eight and twelve when the band started. I. Forced. It. They had no choice but to follow my command."

Mother, why are you doing this?

"This, this, this is *great*," Mac Michaels announced. "Your mom may have just saved the band. I, I can't see how this could be anything but FANTASTIC!"

"And why would you do something so horrible?" the commentator coaxed.

"Because I was ashamed. I was ashamed of my daughter's speech impediment." Her voice choked while tears streamed down her cheeks. "I didn't want my daughter's stutter ruining my reputation and business."

My mother lied. My mother lied to save me. My mother sacrificed herself to save the band. Why would she do that? Why would she do something like that for me?

*   *   *

By eleven-thirty that night, Mother's interview had circuited the late-night news, entertainment shows, and talk shows, making her the most hated woman in the world. While for me, it seemed some of the scattered pieces of my childhood had slid into place.

That's why we never met any of our relatives. That's why Mother always seemed so young and oddly immature. That's why she fabricated lies about her father and why she tried to live in a fictional world where she was important with princess-like values. That's why she had no clue what a mother is supposed to be. I can't imagine being locked in a room or tied to a bed. I can't imagine what she went through being passed around in foster care. I can't imagine the horrors that occurred in the Greenshield home.

*   *   *

Sometime around two forty-five in the morning, Mac called and said vandals torched Victoria's Venus Boutique and Day Spa. It exploded in an inferno and was still burning to the ground. Without hesitating about the time, I called my dad.

"Is she okay?"

"No," Richard confided. "The house has been so quiet. She's missed you girls and Jimmy Jay so much since you left. All she's had is that place. She invested her whole heart into it. Now that it's gone, she's pretty traumatized."

"Dad," I asked. "W-W-Why did she do that?"

"You know why, kiddo."

"But she-she-she ruined her dream."

"For you, kiddo. She did it for you."

And for the first time in my life – as I lay in my beautiful, comfortable bed in my beautiful, spacious condominium – all the anger and animosity I'd harbored throughout the years seemed to disintegrate.

She *loves me. My mother actually loves me.*

And that's when the ironic realization came to me. Something I never imagined. Something that seemed bittersweet at the time but was in some way oddly serene. That night, I called my dad for assurance and kindness and someone to talk to, and – somehow (someway) – found someone I never really knew before. I found my mom.

48

COMING CLEAN

June 9, 2004

T he weather was perfect that day. It's awesome Mother Nature cooperated when I had something so meaningful to say. June 9, 2004, is the day that inspired this journal. It was four days after my mother took the blame for everything that transpired. It's also the day I came clean and apologized to the world. And while doing so, I let everyone know that people with speech disorders are just as intelligent, vulnerable, and fallible as everyone else. We may go through unique experiences, but that doesn't make us different because, in a world of differents, there's no such thing as exactly the same.

"I'm Mitzy McGee," I began, and then I belted out the first few lines of "Millennial Girl" to clear any misconceptions about my singing. And from a makeshift conference platform in the middle of Mac Michaels' crowded driveway, I patched things between Rock Pudding and the world.

"I apologize for w-w-w-what's transpired with my sister being m-m-my speaking voice. That was wrong. This," I paused to collect my bearings, "i-i-is the way I speak."

A few people looked shocked, while the guys in the band stood tall, beaming with pride.

"I have a-a-a speech disorder. A stutter. I went through speech therapy, but-but-but it didn't help me as much as I would have liked. So, this is the way I talk." I leveled my eyes to meet the camera. "G-G-G-Get used to it."

Looking at the crowd, I saw Mac Michaels smile triumphantly as tears streamed from his eyes.

"People with s-s-s-speech disorders are actors, world leaders, doctors, firemen, s-s-s-s-scientists, astronauts, and everything else."

Someone shouted, "You bet!"

"To tell you the truth, I-I don't even see this as a flaw anymore, no-no-no more than I would view a freckle as a flaw, having one toe smaller than the others, or using a device to get around. We, people, bring a variety of s-s-s-skills and variations that make us unique. It's one of-of the great things about humanity."

A murmur came from someone nearby.

"And although my-my mother has taken responsibility for a lot that has happened, I-I-I-I accept my part of the blame and want to apologize to everyone I hurt. I apologize to my band, my-my-my family, and – most importantly – to a-a-anyone anywhere who perceives themselves as being different."

Wearing a royal blue pantsuit (with little makeup and no jewelry or bling), I poured my heart onto television screens worldwide. Behind me were two forces of nature who supported me no matter what: my band-family and my family-family, including my mother and Leiann. Having Mother and Leiann there meant everything to me, especially because they stood side-by-side.

"Life isn't easy."

Someone chuckled.

"It's hard to grow up in a-a-a-a world where you're bullied and don't fit in. B-B-B-But I'm no longer g-g-g-gonna allow bad people and bullies to make me feel less than. I can't do that to myself, and I can't do that to those who have a disorder or any form of special needs.

From now on, I will NOT be ashamed to-to-to speak for myself. Thank you."

Mac walked to the podium to close out the interview when Jimmy Jay stepped up to the mic and made a spontaneous Jimmy Jay-ish statement in his Jimmy Jay-ish way.

"Hey, you all. Just wanted to say judging people for how they talk, walk, hear, skin color, or preferences and beliefs is pretty lame. We're all people here, trying to make the best of life." Jimmy Jay paused for a half-second to take out his man bun; his long, wavy locks tumbled to his shoulders. "One more thing, nobody disrespects my sisters!"

"Okay, okay," Mac Michaels concluded the interview, "that completes this afternoon's press conference. On Thursday, Rock Pudding will return to their previously scheduled tour. I'll keep you posted on concert dates and how and where to purchase tickets. Thank you for...."

*   *   *

Three hours later, the group of us and a slew of party mongers from Mac's crowd celebrated in Mac Michaels' stately backyard.

"These ribs ain't gonna eat themselves," Richard called out, "anyone hungry for some more? Got some veggie kabobs and carne asada here also."

"Oh, heck yeah." Jimmy Jay hoisted himself from the pool and walked over to the grill. "Can't resist your cooking, Pops."

"JJ," Mother gasped. "Your hair's gotten so long. If you'd like me to—"

"Nah," Jimmy Jay cut her off, "some foofy shampoo company is talking about making me their spokesperson." He flipped his long, damp locks, which were truly remarkable. "Thanks, anyway. Maybe you should go after Dad; his hair looks as though it could use a trim. In fact," Jimmy Jay's face scrunched as he gawked at Richard, "I never seen Dad's hair quite so..." He paused, garnering everyone's attention.

"Dad, what's going on? Where's your prison guard cut? How'd you get off work in the middle of the week? And-and you're drinking beer on a weekday. I never seen you—"

Richard turned with his shirt off, displaying his stark white back adorned with a new, terribly placed tattoo.

What's that? Wings? For Baltimore? Dad, why'd you put it there? It's the wrong spot. That's a tramp stamp!

Mother smiled as she walked over to Richard and wrapped her arm around him. "Tell 'em, dear."

"Didn't want to bother you, kids. You're out traveling the world, having all that fun and adventure. But—"

Don't say you're getting another tattoo!

"WHAT!?!" Marnie cut in.

"I retired."

Everyone gasped. No one expected anything like that. It felt as though the earth skidded to a stop. I never knew my father as anything but a correctional officer.

"You-you-you what?"

"I retired. I'm done. Finito. Kaput. I did my time, reached the age of pension parole, and earned my status as an official retiree."

"Tell 'em the other news," Mother urged.

"Gonna save up and buy me a boat."

"Not that news," Mother edged, "the other—"

"Your mother and I are gonna pay the world back for all our blessings. We've decided to sign up for classes to become CASA (court-appointed advocates for youth in the foster system). We're gonna help a lot of kids."

*　　*　　*

We stayed at the pool, having a good time – reminiscing, eating, and catching up on events – when Mac's side gate opened, and a pair of gorgeous men strolled into the backyard.

"Hey, Tommy and Dan," Mac called to them, "glad you could make it."

I turned, and my breath stuck. My knees wobbled, and – for the first time in a couple of years – my kidneys felt like they'd act up again.

Within seconds, I was face to face with Tommy Townsend. Fricking Tommy Townsend.

"Hey, sunflower," Tommy greeted.

He still calls me sunflower. I tried to look inconspicuous as I adjusted my bikini, ensuring no fat globs or embarrassing thingamajigs lobbed out.

"Ah-ah-ah, hey," I greeted as I smiled at the both of them.

"I'd like to introduce you to my brother," Tommy announced. "Dan, here, is my road dog, sidekick, and best friend rolled into one."

"H-H-Hi." I smiled at Dan. *They have the same noses and height.*

"Ahhhhhh, hey," Dan bashfully returned, and I surmised he had a form of autism.

"Dan, your brother, Tommy here, says-says you are my biggest fan. Is-is-is that true?"

Dan glanced to the side as he gave a little nod.

"Well then, I must be the-the-the luckiest girl in the world to have a f-f-f-fan like you."

Tommy's eyes gleamed towards his brother, reflecting an ocean of love.

"I mean it. A lot of fans cut me off and set me loose when they learned I had a-a-a stutter, but not you."

Dan blushed bashfully. "You're my favorite astronaut hero fighter lady."

"Thanks. I'm grateful you-you-you think so."

And then the three of us sat around a table in Mac's fancy backyard in Mac's big fancy chairs and shared stories and laughs. Richard grilled food and showed a laid-back, tatted, uncorrectional side. My mother sat in a corner with Leiann, listening to my sister's stories of helicopter landings and assorted feats she accomplished as a Marine. Marnie cannonballed into the pool, splashing everyone. Billy and Jaslene stood hand in hand, with her belly displaying the first signs of a baby bump, which was obvious but still supposed to be a secret. And Chris Lee, 2-Tall, and Jimmy Jay stood around, laying out ideas for upcoming tracks. As all this wonderful stuff happened, the stars, the moon, and the heavens shined down on all of us as I – Mitzy McGee – finally accepted the person I'd fought since I was small. Myself.

My entire life, I beat myself up and tormented myself for my stutter. I never thought I was good enough to have friends or be accepted by my mom. Even though I was a rock star, I defined myself as a loser who couldn't speak right. And at that moment, I realized I was okay with my nerdish, super-geeky book ways. I was okay with the fact I hadn't grown out of my stutter. I was okay with me.

SECTION VI

AGE TWENTY-NINE

49

POODLE PUCKER

February 5, 2011

Three fifty-two on a crisp, wintery afternoon – after months of preparation, planning, and practice – I looked down at the crowd and estimated Levi's Stadium had around 75,000 anxious spectators.

"I got this," I assured Marnie and Leiann as I prepared to crawl out of the hovering helicopter. "Just keep her steady."

Leiann, a commercial pilot (who'd long since left the Marines), owned a fleet of three of the magnificent flying birds she used to cart customers around as well as perform fire and people rescue.

That, I surmise, is one of the bene's of being a rock star and movie star — the money. Not only did I finance Leiann's McGee Family Rescue, but I paid off my parent's house and bought my dad a modest little fishing boat that we all called the "boat," even though it qualified as being a yacht. My mom wasn't interested in rebuilding Victoria's Venus Boutique and Day Spa, so I bought her a fancy massage chair to flatten her fat globs and cellulite in the convenience of her room.

I also invested in Vanessa Santorini's Italian restaurant, Miss Ocampo's speech camp, and I bought the choir at St. Thomas Baptist a state-of-the-art bus so Miss Mayme and Miss Ruby traveled to gigs in comfort and style. That's the true advantage of being a rock star and striking it big: helping people. There are others I aided and supported; however, I still have a neat little nest egg stashed for the future.

The guys were wise with their money, also. Chris Lee opened a clothing store in 2003; it barely made a profit when he came up with the greatest idea. Using the video footage from Breaking Benjamin Pane (two and a half hours of embarrassing butt shots), he whittled his merchandise to briefs that fit right, making a ton of money. Chris is known as a famous musician and "the seamless butt guy."

2-Tall received his master's (which made his mother ecstatic) and became an activist for human rights. He dated a few fashion models (and a snooty soap opera star) but ended up with a girl he knew and trusted since childhood — Luella Farnsworth. Dr. Luella Farnsworth. Together they have three top-grossing novels on how to make the world a better place and four children who, I assume, keep them on their toes.

Billy, Jaslene, and their kids spend a lot of time raising awareness about the plight of Native Americans and the need for improved education and health care. Although I'm close with both, Jaslene is still my band sister and best friend.

And Jimmy Jay – my super annoying, big-hearted brother – signed on (and invested) with a hair company that has since become a top-grossing beauty stock in the NYSE. If you ever run into the long-haired, loveable beach bum on shores or margarita stands around the world, you'd be hard-pressed not to recognize the world's friendliest billionaire by his beautiful voluminous mane.

*   *   *

Marnie's journey into a seat in the helicopter is quite a tale. After Lou Greenshield shattered our lie, Marnie enrolled in college with the aspiration of attending dental school. Halfway through her second semester, she took a public speaking class and changed her major. The professor of that class, Olé Aikman, turned out to be our one-time mentor from when we started the band. Olé shaved his beard and covered his spider tattoo in a Shakespearian caricature. With Olé's mentorship and advice, Marnie ventured into journalism, eventually earning an award for an editorial piece about a homeless doctor.

* * *

And that's what brings me back to the helicopter at the Super Bowl. Marnie sat next to me in the cabin as Leiann piloted the controls.

"Okay," Marnie suggested, "as they hoist you down, you gotta stay away from your uptight poodle expression. This'll be live-streamed all over the world, and I don't want you scaring any children."

"What are you-you talking a-about? I never look uptight, I-I--"

"That's it!" Marnie pointed out. "That screams uptight poodle. Don't make that face; your mouth, it—"

"Four minutes till you're out the door," the co-pilot cut in. "Just be safe; the future of McGee Rotor Tours is on the line."

"I-I-I know that! I-I-I'm gonna be-be--"

"The laughingstock of the country if you don't do something about that stain on your right boob."

"What!?!" I looked down and saw that someone (presumably one of Leiann's sons) spilled fruit punch on the bodice of my dress. It probably happened before we took flight.

"Shoot!" Leiann gushed. "We're down to three minutes."

"I got this," Marnie declared. She reached into her bag and procured a tube of lipstick.

"What are you-you-you gonna do?"

"Remember that time on the *VMAs* when you wore a heart on your chest." She twisted the tube open. "You had one on Millennial Girl also."

"Yeah."

"Well, I'm gonna—"

Marnie outlined a lipstick heart over the punch stain.

"Two minutes," Leiann cut in, "and thirty-two seconds."

"Dang," Marnie grimaced, "I made one side bigger than the other. Now I gotta fill in a little over here and..."

*   *   *

Two minutes later, I tried to look graceful as the safety rig slowly lowered me to the ground.

"Bye, you guys. Love you." And then I thought about it and relaxed my smile. "P-P-Poodle power!"

"And here she goes, ladies and gentlemen," Marnie broadcasted to television screens and the massive monitor posted at the head of the stadium. "Mitzy McGee begins her descent. I'm telling you folks, this sister of ours (the camera spanned to Leiann and back) is one of the greatest songbirds of all time."

*   *   *

My anxiety dissipated as the cable made a slow, glorious descent.

It's taken a lot to get here. I'm at the Super Bowl! I'm singing in the half-time show at one of the world's greatest spectacles. Look, the choir's on stage. I know Miss Mayme's there with Miss Ruby, Mrs. Meyers, and beautiful Shanice. They've been here for me and backed me with the Stuttering Foundation and the Special Olympics. These are my friends, my fantastic friends, who've joined me on my pilgrimage to make life better.

Look, there's my band. My guys are there too. My brothers. My bandmates. My friends. It took so much hard work to get here, but I couldn't have done it without them. It seems every day of my life has been like that first time the guys took me bike riding. They had my back. No matter how much I messed up or embarrassed them, they've always had my back. With bandmates and brothers like that, I'm probably the luckiest girl in the world.

The moment my feet touched the ground, a crew of technicians unhitched the rescue hook from my harness. I waved goodbye to Marnie as Leiann brought the copter into a lift and then took flight across the sky. The lights in the stadium dimmed, and a halo of spotlight accompanied me to the stage. And then I recalled Richard's advice about releasing my songbird and giving them a good show.

I took my place on stage, surrounded by my bandmates and brothers, my backup dancers, and the choir. Everything went silent.

And then I grabbed the mic, turned to Jimmy Jay, and excitedly announced, "Let's do this!"

* * *

Navigating the freeway from San Francisco to Bakersfield could only be described as a dream. That's because I sat behind the wheel in Mac Michaels' fantastic present for me: the "screaming chicken" itself — a 1977 Pontiac Trans Am. With the tee top off and the wind blowing my hair, I thought about Mac and how lucky we were to be signed by a guy who never let us down. In fact, once he got to know Richard and saw what a great father he was, Mac's the one who insisted we do a song about stepfathers who step up as Dads.

"My Real Dad" promoted the positive perception of step-parenting. Every time we performed that song, we pulled some unassuming, regular schmo from the audience who had no clue what was about to transpire. Then – as his son or daughter presented him with flowers and a card (that included a thousand-dollar gift card, compliments of Rock Pudding) – we displayed moving images of him as our backdrop. The images were funny, heart-warming, sometimes embarrassing, and always heroic. No matter how hard I tried to remain strong, that song always brought me to tears. It's just nice to know they're a lot of real dads in the world.

* * *

I entered the familiar friendly territory of Silvercreek, needing to stretch my legs for a few minutes before I ventured back out on the road.

"Mitzy! Darling!" Mother rushed to the driveway to greet me. She wore no makeup, had her hair in a mom-bun, and her shirt was speckled with food stains. "You're here! You're here! I'm so glad you made it okay."

Gazing up at the window of my old room, I saw the blinds crumpled to the side. Two little faces peered down with inquisitive curiosity.

"Is that them?"

"Yes, darling," she excitedly gushed. "As I explained, that's why we couldn't make it to the show. I've been their court advocate for years," her voice cracked as her eyes misted over. "When, when I found out their foster family just dumped them like that..."

As we walked into the house, her tears subsided. "I'm going to do right by them," she assured. "I promise."

"I-I-I know, Mom."

I gazed around the living room and saw everything in place. The room was immaculate while the aroma of pot roast and Brussels sprouts lingered in the air. Most importantly, on the fireplace mantel, Sarah McGee's porcelain pony overlooked the room in perfect dignity. My mother used nearly all the insurance payoff from the fire to purchase it back from the retired librarian who lived down the street.

I started up the stairs, remembering the thousands of times I journeyed those steps when I lived there. And then I stood at the open threshold of my old room, finding Richard in his grandmother's rocker with a book on his knee. On the bunks, two adorable curly-haired munchkins hid beneath the covers.

"Hi," I greeted.

"They're a little shy, kiddo. But they're happy you're here."

"Ahhh," I responded, "did-did-did you two have a nice dinner?"

Hidden beneath the covers, I saw their heads motion *yes*.

"Did you get the pajamas and the slippers I g-g-g-got you?"

They shook their heads yes again.

"Do you like the mural?"

They shook their heads yes. And then, slowly and timidly, they uncovered themselves so they could check me out.

"Are you the person who did that?" Ashanta asked.

"No," I smiled, "but this used to-to be my room."

They regarded me as they shook their heads again.

"And this mural. This b-b-big, beautiful mural that-that-that covers the walls with all those images and imagination. Well, for me, it was-was-was like a magical barrier of protection. Inside this room, I always felt safe."

"I feel safe here," Ashanta declared.

"Me too," Dee Dee chimed.

"Good," I replied.

I tried to be strong. I tried to hold back my tears. It took all my strength to look at them and not let my heart wallow in sadness. My mother told me how these sisters' parents had died back-to-back of heart disease and cancer, and these girls had been through a lot by being passed around in the system. My mother had already gone through years of counseling to become a CASA. To elevate her status and become a temporary foster parent, my mother took a battery of classes, passed a psychological background, and went to counseling to remediate the shadows of abuse from her childhood. She dedicated eighteen months to providing the girls with a safe home.

"Mitzy," Richard stood from the chair, offering me the storybook, "would you like to have the honor?"

"Yeah, Dad..." I smiled as I gazed into this man's eyes. This man who never raised his voice to me or harmed me. This man who supported me through thick and thin and did what he could to make me feel special. This man who raised me to have values, character, backbone, and respect. This man who had been the world's greatest father even though when he adopted me, I was a scrawny wisp of a girl who didn't smell right or appreciate his kindness.

"Sure."

I accepted the book, settled into the chair, and started reading, knowing full and well I would always look after and care for my new little sisters. But I wouldn't have to worry about their wellbeing, not with my mother and Richard on watch.

* * *

An hour and a half later, I sped south along the 99. As the golden bird on the hood navigated the asphalt highway to my hilltop mansion bungalow in Beverly Hills, my cell phone started to ring.

"Hello, Bud," I greeted when I recognized the name on the caller ID, "how'd it go today?"

"Great," Dan answered, "but I miss you many, many bunches. Tommy can't wait till he finishes this movie and we get to come home. I want to see you so bad. I want to go bike riding, visit the big tree park, and watch goofy laugh movies."

"T-ten more days," I announced, "and Tommy will be done. We'll all b-be together again."

"Like a family," Dan chimed.

I twisted the wedding ring on my finger. "L-L-Like a family."

Tommy was everything I wanted in a man. He accepted me, all of me, every perfect and imperfect part of me. He was funny, fun to be around, loyal, and kind. He knew how to make a mean macaroni and cheese. He laughed at Richard's jokes. He called me "sunflower," even when I was tired and grumpy. And he looked smoking-hot without a shirt.

I thought about it and added, "I know he's asleep, but can you whisper to-to your brother that I-I-I love him."

"I will! I will do that. I can do that for you, Mitzy!" And then Dan's tone changed as he barked, "And no more climbing out of helicopters for you!"

"Okay," I chuckled. "No more helicopter climbs for me. And-And-And, Dan…"

"Yeah?"

"When you get-get-get home, I've got a-a surprise for the both of you."

After I hung up, I rubbed my belly, shifted the Trans Am into overdrive, and gave the gas pedal a little nudge.

"C'mon Sarah," I announce to the eight-week-old baby inside me, "let's see what this feisty little beast can do!"

The end

9 780578 862125